If you love courtr
drawn in with *Rai*

A murder among the ᴇ..ᴛᴇ puts Bob and Marcus in a game of cat and mouse most deadly. *Rain* is a classic courtroom mystery even Perry Mason would applaud. Every detail of the investigation and trial is expressed through narration, action, and intriguing characters. This mystery will captivate readers until the very last page. The foreshadowing is subtle yet brilliant.

The mystery itself is well-plotted—the tension is taut—the reader is thrown into the investigation. The ending caught me by surprise. A brain teaser leaving the reader wanting more. Well done.

From Oberlin Prof. Emerita Sandra Sagarell

Shade, Fault Line, and now *Rain*. If you're not yet a fan of H.N. Hirsch's "Marcus and Bob Mystery" series, you should be. These smart, accomplished, and very believable men, who become a couple in *Shade*, combine their skills and knowledge, Marcus as a college professor and Bob as a lawyer, as they untangle the webs of intrigue that surround murder.

Each book engages with major contemporary issues: the toxic culture of an elite university, the corruption of political ambition, the sleaziness of the sex-for-hire economy. All three books feature terrific writing and great pacing along with accomplished characterization. Hirsch deftly develops Marcus and Bob's domestic and emotional life as both separate from and enmeshed in their sleuthing, and he weaves in their relationships with their friends, Bob's family, their colleagues, and various unsavory academics, politicians, and lawyers.

... Bob decides to defend Marcus's graduate student Kenny against the charge of having murdered his girlfriend Cathy, an acting student, and Marcus and Bob—and we—keep trying to figure out what's a performance and what isn't. Bob has to wrestle with ethical problems to which there are no clear solutions, and *Rain* ends on a cliffhanger which poses questions about justice.

—Sandra A. Zagarell,
Donald R. Longman Professor of English Emerita at Oberlin College

What writers and reviewers say about H.N. Hirsch's first two Bob & Marcus mysteries, *Shade* & *Fault Line*

Hirsch weaves his tale well, capturing Southern California ambience and the interplay of his characters cinematically.
—Grady Harp of Goodreads

Five-star reviews of *Fault Line* from buyers on Amazon

Fault Line is a suspenseful and utterly gritty crime fiction book. . . . Thoroughly satisfying. —the Onlinebookclub.com

Written in the classic style of James Ellroy, *Fault Line* is a murder mystery you won't soon forget. With a full cast of characters, a scenic setting, plus a laundry list of suspects, I couldn't stop reading until the dramatic conclusion. Fans of *L.A. Confidential* will enjoy this political murder mystery. 5+ stars! —N. N. Light's Book Heaven

Libraries and readers looking for a classic gay murder mystery steeped in California culture, political subterfuge, and characters that live on the line of lies and danger will find *Fault Line* a fine study in intrigue ... packed with social and political as well as psychological and relationship insights. Hirsch brings to life a myriad of characters that swirl around this unique murder case and its accompanying special interests. A memorable, compelling read. . . .
— Diane Donovan, *Midwest Book Review*, Donovan's Bookshelf

Bob and Marcus are a gay Nick and Nora, a couple you'll want to spend time and solve mysteries with. —Jean Redmann, author of the award-winning Micky Knight Mystery Series

I loved *Shade* and wondered if author H N Hirsh could meet the same high standard. I shouldn't have worried. *Fault Line* was just as good, and just as fresh. This time we're immersed in law and politics in California, as Bob, now a lawyer, has to figure out the twists and turns of ambition, corruption, and secrets that result in a murder and authorities' resistance to discovering the perpetrator. Well-written and engrossing, *Fault Line* is a must-read for everyone who loves thrillers. —"SMZ" on Amazon

Move over. Bob is driving! Hirsch's second mystery (*Fault Line*) is better than his first! Keep them coming! —KB on Amazon

Five-star reviews of *Shade* from buyers on Amazon

"The Thin Man" goes to Harvard! This is a remarkable first novel which I read in one sitting. Good stuff. A young assistant professor buffeted about by the whims of senior colleagues in the Harvard Government Department circa the 1980s finds redemption and adventure in the midst of murder and scandal in Maine and Massachusetts. The gay romance part reminds me of the old 1930s *Thin Man* films.
—Michael A. Mosher on Amazon

Shade is part murder mystery, part romance novel, part travelogue, and a delight to read. Murder is gruesome business, especially when it involves a young man in the prime of life, but Hirsch excels in tempering harsh reality with pleasant characters, summertime on the New England coast, academic intrigue and, perhaps best of all, a charming tale of two people falling in love.
—Anthony Bidulka, author of
the Merry Bell P.I. trilogy and *Going to Beautiful*
winner of Crime Writers of Canada Best Crime Novel

A jolly good murder mystery, stylishly rendered with a swift-moving plot and loads of local color. Fans of the British murder mystery and LGBTQ romance/mystery genres will find much to savor here. I devoured it in a single session while flying across the Atlantic, passing the time much more enjoyably than with the airline's on-board entertainment!
—Wayne A. Cornelius on Amazon

Fun & intelligent! I love keeping up with this couple, and I learn something new with every mystery they solve. —Linda S. on Amazon

A fabulous gripping mystery, plus a love story. A terrific read! I have become very fond of Bob and Marcus (from the first book in this series, *Shade*). Just as they arrive in San Diego Bob is dragged into a murder investigation. There's all kinds of intrigue and plot twists, and, in the process, a vivid portrayal of San Diego, both gay and straight. Well narrated, great characters! Kept me turning pages to discover who done it. —Priscilla Long on Amazon

In *Shade*, Hirsch writes beautifully and immediately draws you into a world of Harvard, old money, gay romance, and murder most foul. The narrative drives forward almost effortlessly, and is punctuated by one plot twist after another. Can't wait for the next book in the series!
—KB on Amazon

<u>Could not put it down!</u> I am not a regular reader of mysteries. Yet, when I picked up this book, I could not put it down. The author's attention to detail, familiarity with the southern California setting, and knowledge about law & police investigations held my attention and kept me guessing about the identity of the murderer. . . Highly recommended.
—CE Smith on Amazon

Loved the ongoing story of Marcus and Bob, begun in the first book of this series, *Shade*. —An Amazon reader

A mature gay couple, a complex political drama, and descriptions of San Diego that made me want to move to CA. This book is a joy!
—"Inquiring Mind" on Amazon

Pisgah Press was established in 2011 to publish and promote works of quality offering original ideas and insight into the human condition and the world around us.

Copyright © 2023 Harry N. Hirsch

Published by Pisgah Press, LLC
PO Box 9663, Asheville, NC 28815
www.pisgahpress.com

Book design: A. D. Reed, MyOwnEditor.com
Cover design: Martin Phillips

All rights reserved. No part of this publication may be reproduced, stored in a retrieval system, or transmitted, in any form or by any means, electronic, mechanical, photocopying, recording, or otherwise, without the prior written permission of Pisgah Press, except in the case of quotations in critical articles or reviews.

This is a work of fiction. All the characters and events portrayed in this book are either products of the author's imagination or are used fictitiously.

Library of Congress Control Number: 2023951958
Library of Congress Cataloging-in-Publication Data
Rain/H.N. Hirsch

ISBN: 978-1-942016-84-7
First Edition
May 2024
Printed in the United States of America

Rain

H. N. Hirsch

Pisgah Press
Asheville, NC

I had failed to imagine, I had not understood.
—Joan Didion

1

"Professor George, I think I'm about to be arrested for murder."

Marcus had just finished his lecture, loosened his tie, and was about to walk back to his office. He stepped outside into yet another perfect late afternoon in Southern California, temperature in the low 70s, warm sun, crisp breeze off the ocean. He inhaled. The campus sat on a bluff overlooking the Pacific, and the smell and feel of the ocean was always in the air. Marcus never got tired of it. Natives took the weather for granted, but Marcus didn't; he grew up in Chicago, in the snowbelt.

He was looking forward to the drive home and changing into shorts. He hated wearing a jacket and tie, but felt he needed it in large lecture courses like this one, "Ethics," a required course for first-year students in Earl Warren College, one of the several undergraduate colleges that made up the gigantic University of California, San Diego. Most of the students, almost all in their first year, resented the requirement, and Marcus learned quickly that he needed all the professorial authority he could muster. Marcus didn't much like the course either; he didn't think "Ethics" was a topic that lent itself to lectures. It required nuance, give and take, and the classes, Marcus was convinced, needed to be much smaller; he said as much at several faculty meetings.

But the University of California was a gigantic operation, and the powers that be had long ago decided lecture courses were the only way to manage. By now, in the mid-1990s, the system was firmly cemented in place, and he put up with it.

There wasn't much choice. For an expert on political rhetoric, career opportunities beyond academia did not really exist, unless he wanted to become a political speechwriter, which, he was sure, would be even worse.

He wanted to get home and play with Oscar, the five-year old golden retriever he shared with his partner Bob. Maybe they'd go out to dinner when Bob got home; they were both working hard these days and not much in the mood for cooking.

Kenny Glick, one of his graduate students, was waiting for him on a bench outside.

Marcus stared at him, stunned silent.

"Professor George?"

"Kenny, is this a joke?"

"I wish. I've just been questioned by the police. I think I'm about to be arrested for murder."

2

Marcus kept himself calm. Kenny was one of his academic advisees; he was studious, quiet, smart. He had just passed his general exams and was beginning to work on his dissertation topic. Most students took a few months off after their generals before starting to work on the next big thing, but Kenny dove right in. He was ambitious, and Marcus admired him for it.

"Come back to the office with me."

During the short walk across the quadrangle and taking the elevator up to Marcus's office on the fourth floor of the concrete monstrosity known as HSS, the Humanities and Social Sciences Building, neither of them spoke. Several of the students they met in the halls waved or smiled at Marcus, and though he did his best to smile back and look normal, he felt anything but.

Marcus tried to organize his thoughts as he opened the door to his office. They both sat, and Marcus turned on the desk lamp and waited. He couldn't imagine what this was about, and then he remembered: The undergraduate woman who had been murdered.

"Is this about Cathy?" Marcus asked. He kept his voice as calm as he could.

"Yes."

Cathy Yaeger had been a senior majoring in Theater. Marcus knew her slightly because she had acted in some of the productions at Diversionary, a local LGBT theater group where he sat on the board of directors. She was strikingly beautiful, with short, black hair and blue eyes, and she was quite talented, with a silky voice that reminded Marcus of Jane Fonda. She had died, tragically, a few weeks before, and the papers said it was accidental death but gave few details. Everyone at Diversionary was devastated, and the story dominated the local news cycle for days.

"Did you even know her?"

"Yes. We were dating. Casually."

That was a surprise. Marcus had thought Kenny might be gay, although he didn't know for sure and they never discussed it. And then he remembered Kenny had been at one of Diversionary's closing night parties, although as far as he could remember, he and Cathy showed no signs of being a couple. In fact, he seemed to remember Kenny flirting with someone else.

"It was an accident, wasn't it? Or at least, that's what was announced."

"I know," Kenny replied. "But now they're saying there's new evidence. And the police think I did it."

3

Marcus didn't know what to say, or do. He made a quick decision.

"Can you come home with me? My partner is a lawyer. He'll know what to do. Have you spoken to a lawyer yet? Did you have one with you when you talked to the police?"

"No. They just showed up at my door and started asking questions. I was completely surprised. Shocked, really. I answered their questions." He hesitated. "I don't have anything to hide."

Marcus knew that it was probably a mistake to talk to the police at all without a lawyer present, but he didn't say so. Kenny was so young, it made sense that he wouldn't have known what to do or not do.

"They didn't arrest you?"

"No. They just told me not to leave town."

"Okay. Let's go. Do you have a car here?"

"No, I took the shuttle from Hillcrest."

The UCSD Hospital was located in Hillcrest, down in the center of San Diego, and there was a shuttle bus up to the main campus in La Jolla, about 12 miles away. Lots of students lived in Hillcrest, a lively, walkable, and bohemian neighborhood, and rode the shuttle. Marcus and Bob, his partner of many years, lived in the nearby neighborhood of Normal Heights.

"Okay. Give me a few minutes, I have to make a few calls, and then we'll go. Can you wait for me downstairs?"

"Thanks, Professor George." Most graduate students called faculty members by their first names, but for some reason Kenny always called them "Professor."

Kenny looked relieved. Marcus noticed a thin ribbon of sweat on his brow.

After Kenny left, Marcus just sat. He didn't need to make any calls but did want a few minutes to calm down. He stared out his narrow window with its a partial view of the ocean.

He realized he had better call Bob, tell him what had happened.

A criminal defense attorney in solo practice, Bob had started out as an Assistant District Attorney for the city, but that had only lasted a few months, when he quit in disgust at a major scandal involving his boss, DA Fred Stevens. The scandal never hit the papers and Stevens was still in office.

When he left, Bob had looked around at various corporate and law firm jobs but decided in the end to go solo, much as his father in Connecticut had done before him. It took a while, but Bob slowly built up his practice and it was now thriving. He and Marcus had struggled financially for a few years, and had finally, reluctantly, sold the Kandinsky that Marcus had inherited from the family of one of his previous students—a student murdered when Marcus was a young assistant professor at Harvard. The painting had brought in a fortune, and they were able to use what they needed for living expenses for a few years and still sock away a bundle in investments. For their old age, Bob had joked.

"Unless, of course, I leave you for a younger man," Bob had smirked. Marcus was ten years older, and Bob teased him about it whenever he knew it wouldn't really upset him.

Sarah, Bob's secretary, picked up on the second ring. She was no nonsense, kind, and unbelievably efficient. Both men considered her a good friend.

"It's Marcus. Is he there?"

"Yep, hold on." She transferred the call.

Marcus told him what had happened.

Bob sighed. "I don't know, Pinky, if I can take the case. I'm kinda swamped. And I don't have that much experience with murder cases."

They had taken to call each other "Pinky" after watching Spencer Tracy and Katherine Hepburn do the same in *Adam's Rib*. Both stars played lawyers, on opposite sides of a case. It was one of Bob's favorite movies and they had watched the video at least once a year. They could almost recite the dialogue by heart. Bob had studied film as an undergraduate at Brown, and when they had first gotten together, a decade before, he had taken it upon himself to show Marcus all the movies he had missed.

"I know. But at least you could give him some advice," Marcus said hopefully, making it sound like a question. "And maybe refer him to someone if you need to. I had no idea what to say."

Bob sighed again. "I guess. Okay. I'll meet you both at home."

Marcus grabbed his briefcase, stuffing in some material he needed to read that evening, turned out the light, and collected Kenny. They walked the short distance to the vast parking lot.

To live is to park, Marcus had told Bob's parents when they asked what it was like living in Southern California.

"Better not say more about what happened until we talk to Bob," Marcus said.

Kenny nodded. They were silent as they drove. Kenny stared out the window of Marcus's Honda Civic as they zipped past Mount Soledad and Mission Bay. He seemed lost in thought.

They both were.

4

Bob and Jason had just walked in the front door, and they left it open when they saw Marcus's car pull up. Jason, a former cop, tall, blond, and gorgeous, was Bob's investigator and one of their best friends. They often called him "Tab" since he looked so much like Tab Hunter, the 1950s, secretly gay Hollywood heartthrob. Jason had been the first openly gay detective on the San Diego police force. Bob had met him when he first worked for the DA and had convinced him to leave the force and work in Bob's practice.

They settled around the dining room table, with Oscar, their retriever, wagging his tail wildly and going from person to person, wanting everyone to pet him. Marcus finally pulled him away and let him out into the back yard. That was the thing about golden retrievers; they instantly loved everyone. Their house had once been burgled, and they were convinced Oscar had wagged his tail, licked the guy, and led him straight to the TV and computers, which were missing when they got home. Luckily the police had quickly recovered everything.

They had been in their house for five years, and they had come to love it, and the neighborhood, which they had chosen because it was called Normal Heights, which they thought hilarious when they first heard it. It was close to Hillcrest, the center of gay San Diego, and near several major freeways.

"All right," Bob said. "We need this conversation to be covered by attorney-client privilege, even if I don't end up as your lawyer. You need to sign this document. And Marcus, you need to sign this, indicating that you are working for me as an investigator; that way, anything you hear, or anything Kenny told you, is privileged. It's fishy, because you don't really work for me, but we may get away with it if anyone asks questions, which they won't. Kenny, you'll need to pay me a nominal sum for this conversation, and Marcus, I'll pay you a salary. Don't expect much."

Everyone chuckled as the documents were signed.

"Don't worry about the fees," Kenny said. "My parents will cover expenses."

Marcus realized he didn't know anything about Kenny's background, except that he had grown up in Los Angeles and had been an undergraduate at Stanford, where he excelled and graduated with honors.

"Okay, good. Now tell me everything, from the beginning, starting with your relationship with this young woman. Don't leave anything out. How did you meet?"

Both Bob and Jason took notes. Marcus went to the kitchen, mixed a pitcher of lemonade, and put pretzels into a bowl. He came back to the dining room quickly.

The story sounded straightforward to Marcus. Kenny had met Cathy at a party about two years before and they started dating. They lived near each other in Hillcrest. Both had their own rooms in apartments they shared with other UCSD students. Kenny often stayed over at Cathy's place, which, he said, was larger and nicer.

"The initial reports implied she died of an overdose. Do you know, did she take sleeping pills, or sedatives of any kind?" Bob asked.

"I don't know." Kenny hesitated, then said, "I saw her take a pill sometimes, but I didn't know what they were."

"And you never asked her?"

"No."

"And did you know she drank? Did you drink together?"

Again, Kenny hesitated. "We sometimes drank a little. Shared a bottle of wine with food, that kind of thing. I didn't think she was a heavy drinker."

"Did she ever seem drunk?"

"Not drunk, no. Tipsy maybe."

"And your relationship was intimate?"

"Yes." Kenny looked down.

"Okay. Now tell me about the interview with the police."

Oscar scratched at the kitchen door. Marcus got up, let him in, and poured dog food into his bowl, which he gobbled down before lying down next to the dining room table. Marcus reached down and scratched his ear. Oscar always calmed down after he ate.

"They just showed up at my apartment yesterday morning. Two detectives."

"Did you get their names?" Jason asked.

Kenny took a piece of paper out of his pocket.

"Yes. Bobbitt and Rosen."

Bob looked over at Jason, who pursed his lips. They both knew Bobbitt from Bob's brief stint at the DA's office, and didn't think much of him. Rosen, Jason surmised, was new, and neither of them knew him.

"What did they ask? Recount the conversation as carefully as you can."

"They started out by saying that the investigation of Cathy's murder had been reopened. I asked why, and they said that new evidence had come to light. That's all they said about it. Then they asked me about our relationship, had we been together that night, what we had done, that kind of thing."

"Had you been together?"

"Yes. I told them. We had met up for a drink around six-thirty, then went back to Cathy's place. We ordered a pizza. We watched a movie. We went to bed around midnight."

"Did you drink?"

"We had martinis at the Brass Rail, then shared a bottle of wine with the pizza."

The Brass Rail was a gay bar in Hillcrest that a lot of straight students frequented as well—in part because the drinks were cheap. It was near where they both lived. Both Bob and Jason noticed that this meant that they mixed grape and grain, gin or vodka in a martini and then wine, which makes some people really drunk. In fact it made some people ill.

"Did Cathy take any medication before bed?"

"I don't know. She did go into the bathroom."

"Did you have sex?"

Kenny looked down again. "Yes."

"And in the morning?"

"I got up around six and left to go to the gym. Cathy was asleep."

"And as far as you know, she was still breathing?"

"Yes, of course." Kenny sounded agitated for the first time. "I would have called an ambulance if I thought anything was wrong."

"Okay. I have to ask these questions. What else did the police want to know?"

Marcus could tell Kenny was getting upset.

"They asked if we ever got rough."

"Rough?"

"When we had sex. They asked if we ever had rough sex."

Both Jason and Bob looked up from their notes. Marcus could tell Bob was now treading very carefully.

"And did you?"

Kenny leaned forward. He put his hands on the dining room table. He took a swig of lemonade.

"No. I mean, we horsed around a little, sometimes, but no, nothing too kinky."

"Horsed around?"

"Do I need to draw pictures?"

"Kenny, no, but I need to know this. What exactly do you mean?"

Marcus thought at this point Kenny was trying hard to keep his voice even.

"We horsed around. Some slapping, that kind of thing. Nothing dangerous or crazy."

"Did you tell the police that?"

"No. I just said we had a normal, healthy sexual relationship. Which is the truth."

"Did you do any of that that night?"

"No."

"Okay, what else did they ask?"

"That was about it. They told me not to leave town and that they would be in touch."

"One more thing. Have you ever been arrested?"

"No. Not even a parking ticket."

5

Kenny said he needed to use the bathroom, and Marcus showed him where it was. When he came out Marcus looked at his watch; it was 6:30 and he knew everyone must be getting hungry.

"So," Kenny asked Bob, "can you take my case?"

"First, we don't know if there is a case. The police interview may have been routine."

"It didn't feel like it." Kenny stifled a nervous laugh.

"Well, it never does. We'll take it one step at a time. We'll poke around a bit, try to find out what the police are up to," Bob said, nodding toward Jason, who nodded back. "We should meet at the end of the day tomorrow. Can you come to my office around five?"

Kenny said he could, and Bob gave him the address and directions.

"I'll take you home," Marcus said.

Kenny nodded.

"Give us a minute, I'll be right out."

Kenny gave Oscar a pat on the head and walked out the front door.

"I'll pick up food," Marcus said to Bob and Jason. "What do you feel like?"

"Italian," Bob said. "I'll call in the order."

Marcus walked outside and drove Kenny to his small apartment building in Hillcrest. On the way, neither said anything, but as they approached his place Kenny asked Marcus if he thought Bob would take the case.

"I really don't know. He's pretty booked up right now. But I know he'll help you find someone if he can't do it himself."

Kenny nodded, but looked worried. Marcus felt for him; he really couldn't imagine Kenny as a murderer.

Marcus had learned over his years of teaching to trust his gut when it came to students, especially graduate students—which ones were honest, which weren't; who could be trusted, which ones would crash and burn. Kenny had his shit together, as a colleague of Marcus's had said.

Kenny was planning to write a dissertation on changes within the national Democratic party and its rhetoric, focusing on the Democratic Leadership Council that had catapulted the Clintons to the White House. He was a sharp thinker; he saw the DLC as a betrayal of what Democrats had always stood for, fought for, starting with the New Deal. He was tracing subtle but important changes in rhetoric. The party, he thought, was becoming too centrist, too focused on suburban swing voters and big money donors, not enough on core Democratic constituencies.

And he didn't trust Clinton. He saw him as a con man, almost as bad as Newt Gingrich, who, Kenny was sure, was going to be elected Speaker when the Republicans took the House in the midterms. He saw them both as salesmen, not statesmen, and he thought American politics was changing profoundly as a result.

Politics was no longer about policy, Kenny was convinced; it was all about image. For one thing, Clinton, he thought, was performing the role of faithful husband. Marcus had his own doubts about the Clinton marriage, although he didn't think it mattered. There was JFK, after all. And the Roosevelts. And LBJ. Even Ike.

But in general, Marcus thought, Kenny was onto something about changes in the Democratic Party and changes in how elections were being conducted. And Kenny was good-looking—tall, well-built, with regular features and a winning smile; he had charisma. He had a great future in front of him.

No, he couldn't be a murderer.

"Try not to get too ahead of yourself. From what you've said, it really might have been a routine interview. They always talk to romantic partners and roommates. It makes you an automatic suspect. In fact," Marcus added with a smile, "that's how I met Bob, when his summer roommate was murdered in Maine. The roommate had been my student. A long time ago."

"Really. Wow. You'll have to tell me that story sometime."

Marcus smiled. "Some day. When you finish your PhD."

"Yeah. If I'm not in jail."

Marcus pulled up to his building and Kenny put his hand on the door handle.

"Well, I hope you're right about the police. Thanks for helping me, Professor. I really appreciate it."

Marcus watched him walk slowly up the long stairs to his apartment. Given the climate, lots of small apartment buildings in San Diego has outside stairways. Kenny's shoulders drooped and he looked defeated. The stairs led to a long balcony that stretched across what looked like three apartments.

On the drive home, Marcus stopped for the food Bob had ordered from their favorite Italian restaurant: lasagna and spaghetti, garlic bread, antipasto salad. It smelled great and made Marcus's stomach grumble on the short drive home.

When he got there, Jason was setting the table and Bob was on the telephone in the kitchen. Oscar, as usual, greeted Marcus at the door as if he had been away for weeks.

Bob hung up and walked into the dining room, carrying a bottle of red wine and a corkscrew.

"So . . ." Marcus asked.

"I don't know," Bob said as they sat down. "I really am swamped. Tomorrow I'll see if I can get any information out of the DA's office, and Jason will talk to Bobbitt, try to find out if the police have any actual evidence. They probably won't say, but it doesn't hurt for the cops to know Ken has a lawyer asking questions, at least at this point. Might make them cautious."

Marcus nodded. "What does your gut say?" he asked.

They had once talked about gut instincts; as Marcus trusted his about students, Bob had learned to trust his own about clients and potential clients.

As he dished out the lasagna, he answered, slowly, carefully. "Not sure either way. But it doesn't matter. If he does get charged, what matters is if I can convince one juror he didn't do it."

"But . . ."

"No buts. I'm exhausted. I was in court all morning with a tough judge. Let's eat."

Marcus was surprised by Bob's cut-and-dried attitude, but did as he was told. He dug into his lasagna.

6

As always, Bob was up and gone early the next morning. He loved practicing law, Marcus knew, but he hated the long hours, especially now that he was a solo practitioner. His caseload was growing, and he had to do almost everything himself. He usually had a law clerk or two, recent law school grads looking for experience, but he could only give them so much of the work, and found in some ways they just added to his workload. They had to be instructed, taught the ropes, and their work had to be checked for mistakes. He thought about finding an experienced partner to share the caseload but so far he hadn't done it.

Marcus got up a little later, took Oscar for a short walk, fed him, had a bagel and coffee, and left for campus. He had an undergraduate lecture at 10 o'clock and a department meeting in the afternoon. As usual, Oscar followed him to the door after he dressed and gave him his most pitiful don't-leave-me look.

"Don't look at me like that, you know we'll both be home later. And Penny will be here." Penny was a neighbor and friend they hired to come over and play with Oscar mid-day, whenever both Bob and Marcus were both going to be gone. She was a writer, lived down the block, and worked from home. Oscar adored her.

Just as he was unlocking the door to his campus office, the phone rang. Kenny.

"The police want me to come in for a formal interview. Downtown. What do I do?" He sounded panicked.

What time do they want you there?"

"At four o'clock."

"Ok. Let me call Bob. Call me back in ten minutes."

Marcus dialed Bob's office and Sarah put him through.

"Not a good sign," Bob sighed.

"So will you take his case?" Marcus was beginning to feel a sense of dread.

"I don't know, Pinky. We haven't had time to find anything out. I have no idea what's going on here."

"Well, could you at least go with him to the interview this afternoon? He can't go in there alone. He'll be petrified, he might blurt out something he shouldn't."

There was a long pause.

"Yes, okay. Tell him to call me. He'll need to come in and sign some documents."

"Thanks. Really. I'm worried for him."

"A police interview doesn't necessarily mean he'll be charged. But they must have some kind of evidence. I need to know what it is."

"I know what you always say, anyone can do anything given the right circumstances, and looks can be deceiving. That you never really know what people are capable of. But I can't imagine this kid as a murderer."

"None of this makes sense, at least not yet," Bob agreed. "Young guy, apparently well-off, smart, no priors. And the coroner's first report, accidental death."

"Right."

"But you never know," Bob added.

After Marcus hung up he fetched himself a cup of coffee from the department pot and tried to concentrate on his lecture notes. He got through the lecture, distractedly, and at the afternoon department meeting was barely paying attention as his colleagues fought over . . . something. He cared less and less these days about their squabbles; he just wanted to teach his classes, advise his students, and do his own research—these days a project about the rhetoric of American progressivism at the turn of the twentieth century. But more and more, he had realized, he was going through the motions of his academic life, which didn't work so well at UCSD, a high-powered research campus.

Marcus published a respectable amount of work, got some attention from other scholars and good reviews of his books, but by this point in his career it was clear he would never make it onto the A-list—the scholars who were always read and cited by their colleagues, got invited to give prestigious lectures. Academic stars. He was high on the B list, he knew, not a bad place to be, really, but . . . a bit disappointing. Not just to his colleagues and the administration at UCSD, but to himself as well.

This must be what a mid-life crisis feels like, he had thought to himself one day, sitting alone at his office desk, staring at a graduate student's dissertation draft sitting in front of him, pages he couldn't bring himself to read. He had recently turned 40, and he knew this happens to people. Everything feels routine. Been there, done that.

There were days when he left campus as soon as he could; all he wanted was to go home and cuddle with Oscar until Bob came home, maybe take him to San Diego's dog beach. Oscar loved the water so much it made Marcus feel calm, centered. He didn't even mind the sand that clung to Oscar's fur when they went, which ended up all over the back seat of the car and sometimes in the house when they got home. Some days, instead of the beach, he would take a long nap at home and let Oscar curl up on the bed next to him, even though they had agreed not to let Oscar onto the bed.

"Don't tell Bob," he would always say as he tucked an arm around Oscar's middle, and Oscar let out a murmur and seemed to understand. Of course Marcus knew dogs didn't really understand human language, but he did notice Oscar never tried to get on the bed when Bob was home. That made him smile.

Bob knew Marcus did this, he picked up Oscar's scent on the bedspread, but didn't let on. That made Bob smile too.

7

Kenny went to Bob's office at noon, as instructed, signed the necessary documents, and wrote out a check. The office was in a small building in Mission Hills, a tony neighborhood next to Hillcrest. The building was next to a health food restaurant that Bob patronized when he had the time, but most days he just ate yogurt or a sandwich at his desk. Bob told Kenny that he would act as his counsel for the time being, at least, and make a decision about going forward with the case if and when Kenny was charged.

Kenny said he understood. They arranged to meet in front of police headquarters at 3:30.

Bob then called Billy Lewis, the chief assistant district attorney, whom he knew from his short stint working there. He had Jason make contact with Bobbitt, since they had worked together when Jason was on the force.

Billy and Gus both refused to say much, but they did reveal why the case had been reopened. Cathy's family, unhappy with the San Diego medical examiner's conclusion that Cathy's death had been accidental, had conducted a second autopsy of the body before she was buried. The second examiner found evidence of bruising around her neck and her vagina. He concluded she had been strangled during intercourse.

"Melinda was away, her new, incompetent assistant had done the first autopsy," Bobbitt told Jason. Melinda Ivanov, the city's chief medical examiner, was someone who didn't make mistakes.

The evidence was subtle, the second examiner maintained, but clear, and her family, apparently well-off, was demanding a more thorough investigation. Cathy's father was a Hollywood bigwig, it turned out, a producer at Universal Studios, and very well-connected. Her mother was a former actress who used to do the occasional television role.

"And," Bobbitt told Jason, "we dug into Cathy's background. Let's just say she wasn't exactly a sweet, innocent young girl."

Bob was alarmed. But if, as Bobbitt seemed to imply, Cathy had more sexual partners than just Kenny, the murderer could be any of them. That would offer a clear means of showing reasonable doubt to a jury. Few criminal cases actually went to a jury; most ended up with a plea deal of some sort, usually after all sorts of maneuvering and bargaining. Bob was good at all that but loved jury trials, wished he had more of them. He loved the suspense, the theatricality; it produced a kind of high.

And this case was becoming intriguing.

At 3:30 Bob met Kenny and ushered him into police headquarters. As instructed, Kenny wore a suit and a conservative tie, shoes polished, face scrubbed. The very picture of respectability, a California golden boy.

He will impress a jury, Bob thought to himself.

The interview took place in a small, airless room on the third floor. A secretary showed them into the room that held an old wood table, various chairs, and a two-way mirror. The floor was filthy. After a few minutes Gus Bobbitt and Jeffrey Rosen entered from the opposite side. Bobbitt introduced Rosen, who nodded and gave a slight smile.

"Mister Glick, you said you had spent the night before she was found dead in Cathy Yaeger's bed."

"Yes."

"Did you have sexual relations that night?"

"Yes, we did. We had been seeing each other for a while."

"Did your activity that night involve violence of any sort?"

Kenny looked over at Bob, who gave a slight nod, signaling yes, answer the question.

"No. It did not."

"No?"

"No. It did not." Kenny spoke slowly, and, Bob thought, with a slight touch of defiance.

Bobbitt took photos out of a folder he had carried into the room. He placed them in front of Kenny and Bob. They were shocking: photos from the second autopsy. Bob swallowed hard and Kenny turned white. Bob saw that Cathy had been a very attractive young woman with full breasts and a slim figure.

"As you can see clearly in these photos, Mr. Glick, there are signs of a struggle on Ms. Yeager's neck and around her vagina. How did they get there?"

Kenny paused for a moment. "I have no idea," he said, very quietly.

"Was Ms. Yaeger naked when you had relations that night?"

Kenny hesitated. "Yes."

"And you have no idea how these bruises came to be? You maintain you didn't notice them, or put them there?"

"I did not."

"How many nights in the previous week had you been with Ms. Yaeger?"

Kenny looked away, toward the dirty window covered in wire mesh.

"I'm not exactly sure, maybe three."

"Three?"

"Well we didn't exactly keep a record."

"Were your relations with Ms. Yaeger ever violent in any way?"

"Never anything that would produce that kind of bruising." Kenny pointed to the photos. Bob noticed that his answer was somewhat evasive, and that worried him.

"Mr. Glick, we are arresting you for the murder of Catherine Yaeger."

Rosen then spoke for the first time. "Please stand up Mr. Glick." Kenny did as he was told as Rosen put him in handcuffs and read him the Miranda warnings.

"Hold on, hold on," Bob said.

"Save it counselor," Bobbitt said as Rosen led Kenny out of the room.

8

After Rosen and Kenny left, Bob threw his pen down on the table.

"Gus, for God sake, come on. You told Jason this young woman wasn't an angel. How do you know Kenny created those bruises? And even if he did, that isn't murder."

"There's more. Talk to Billy." Gus nodded toward the two-way mirror, and then Billy Lewis, the assistant DA, came into the room from the door next to the mirror. DAs often watched police interviews, Bob knew; he had done it himself.

"Billy," Bob said, "come on."

"Let's all sit," Billy said, and the three of them sat down. Lewis was carrying a cup of coffee in a paper cup.

"We have witnesses. Glick getting nasty with the deceased in public places. Giving her a lot to drink. Violent arguing. And someone who heard an earful from the deceased about the relationship." Lewis paused. "If I were you, I'd plead this one out."

Bob smirked. He hoped the look on his face telegraphed "thanks, but keep your advice to yourself."

"I will need to see those statements."

"Come back to the office with me, I'll give you the highlights."

"First I need to talk to my client."

God damn it, he was saying to himself. His mind was racing. There wasn't time to find another lawyer, and the police case felt weak. They often moved fast in these cases, Bob knew, hoping to get a plea deal and close the case quickly.

He really didn't want to take on a murder case right now, even if the police case was weak, especially not one involving what looked like a sex crime. Any kind of murder case was hard and exhausting and you felt dirty when it was over, even if you won, even if your client was innocent. Too much darkness.

But he knew Marcus would be upset if he dropped the case, and the police were probably hoping to railroad the kid before he had a good lawyer. The early days of a murder investigation were crucial.

Bob closed his eyes for a moment, and then turned to Bobbitt. "When will he be arraigned?"

"First thing tomorrow morning."

Bob knew Kenny could have been arraigned that evening in night court and set free on bail, but the police wanted him to spend a night in jail—a typical bullying tactic. They wanted to rattle him. Bob had seen the tactic turn quickly into a guilty plea, and it might work with Kenny, who was young and probably scared shitless.

"Okay. I'll talk to him now. Billy, can we meet back in your office in an hour?"

"Sure, counselor. You know where to find me. That place you deigned to work for a few months?" Lewis smirked.

Bob ignored him and headed for the cells to talk to his new client.

9

Bob looked at his watch as he headed for the holding cells; it was now 5:30. He had skipped lunch and his stomach was grumbling, but he needed to see Kenny and then meet with Billy that night, before the arraignment. Once Kenny was formally charged, rules and procedures would apply, and he'd have to wait for the formal discovery process to see what the police had. Tonight, there was a chance Billy would show his cards, or at least some of them.

He took the elevator up to the fifth floor and told the desk officer, a familiar face, that he needed to see his client.

"You know the drill, counselor. Room 4."

Bob walked down the dingy, dark hallway and entered the small meeting room. It smelled of sweat and was completely airless. He loosened his tie.

After a few minutes an officer brought in Kenny, and they sat. Kenny looked terrified. The color was still drained from his face.

"I know this is awful. But tomorrow morning we'll get you out on bail. After I leave here I'll be meeting with the assistant DA handling your case, and have a better sense of the evidence they claim they have."

Kenny nodded. He kept rubbing his fingers, trying to erase the ink traces left from being fingerprinted.

"For now, I need you to tell me more about your relationship with Cathy, especially fights you might have had in public, or in front of other people." Bob was choosing his words carefully.

"Well," Kenny said, after hesitating, "we did sometimes argue. We both had a bit of a temper."

"In front of other people?"

Kenny looked down. "Yeah, sometimes."

"What did you argue about?"

Kenny let out a little laugh, which Bob found strange. "Little stuff, mostly, stupid things. Cathy wasn't the easiest person in the world. I guess I'm not either. But I cared about her. And I didn't kill her." Now he sounded and looked defiant.

"Do you recall any particularly loud arguments?"

Bob wanted to ask about "violent arguments" but thought better of it.

Kenny looked away. "Dunno. Sometimes. We . . . both of us shouted sometimes."

"Where?"

"Around. Parties."

"I'll need any details you can remember. Dates, who was present. Did you drink a lot?"

"Depends on what you mean by 'a lot.'" Kenny let out another strange little laugh.

"Okay. On a typical night out, how many drinks?"

"Three, maybe four."

Bob was surprised but tried not to show it. He remembered what Kenny had said about sharing some wine with food. This didn't square, and Bob wondered, for the first time, if Kenny was telling the whole truth. Then another question popped into his head, one he should have asked the night before.

"Was your relationship exclusive?"

Again Kenny looked down. "No."

"So you saw other people? Did Cathy?"

"Yeah. We both did."

"Is that one of the things you argued about?"

There was a pause. "Sometimes."

"Did you want an exclusive relationship? Did she?"

Another pause. "She did. At least some of the time."

"I'll need the names of other people you were seeing, and, if you know them, the names of people Cathy was seeing."

Kenny got a bit agitated. "Is that really necessary?"

"Kenny, you're about to be charged with murder. This is serious. I need to know everything."

"Okay. I get it. I'll put together a list."

Bob reached into his briefcase and handed Kenny a small pad of blank white paper and a pen.

"Write down any names you know, and anything you can remember about arguments you had in public—who was there, dates, location. I'll get it from you tomorrow."

Kenny nodded. "What will happen tomorrow?"

"You'll be arraigned and formally charged in front of a judge. It's a straightforward process, over quickly. Then there'll be a discussion about bail. I assume, from what you said last night, your family will have the funds to post bail?"

Kenny nodded.

"Once you're out we'll talk again. One more thing. Say absolutely nothing to anyone—anyone in the cells, any of the officers. Not a single word, no matter what anyone says to you. That's really important. And tomorrow, at the arraignment, say nothing, unless the judge asks you a direct question. Try not to show any facial expressions or nervousness. I know that's hard, but it matters."

"Okay."

"Make those lists, and then try to get some sleep. I'll see you first thing in the morning."

10

It was now past 6:00. Bob stopped at a phone booth in the lobby and called Marcus, told him what had happened.

"Oh, God."

"Try not to worry. I have to see Billy Lewis. I'll be late."

"I'm making a casserole. I'll keep it warm. Do you want Jason here when you get home?"

By now Marcus knew how these things went, though he was surprised at how fast the case was moving. And he was worried; if the police were ready to charge Kenny, what the hell was really going on?

"Yeah, give him a call. I should be home in maybe ninety minutes."

On the short drive to the DA's office, Bob opened his glove compartment and took out a granola bar he kept there for times like this. It was hard and stale but he didn't care. He gobbled it down, getting crumbs all over himself, and then took a swig from the water bottle he kept on the passenger seat. It always leaked and got Marcus's pants wet when they went somewhere together in Bob's car, which made Marcus mad and made Bob laugh.

"You're like Lucy with the football," Marcus once grumbled.

He parked and made his way to Billy Lewis's office. The sun was setting and there was a cool breeze off the ocean.

Bob never liked going to the DA's office, given his past history there. He hoped that the late hour meant not too many familiar faces would be around.

He was wrong; as he waited for the elevator in the lobby, Fred Stevens, the DA himself, was standing in the elevator when the doors opened. The last person in the world Bob wanted to see.

Stevens scowled. "Counselor," was all he said as he left the elevator and walked away.

"Good evening," Bob replied, in what he thought of as his professional tone, a balance between polite and icy.

Great, Bob thought. *What a great day this is turning out to be.*

11

Bob found Billy Lewis eating a sandwich and drinking coffee.

"Would you like a cup? Help yourself, you know where it is."

Well, Bob thought, *at least he's being polite.* He sat down in the chair in front of Lewis's desk. It was awful coffee but Bob needed the caffeine.

"So. What sort of evidence do you think you have on my innocent client?"

Lewis smiled and opened a folder on his desk.

"You've seen the photos from the second autopsy. Turned out Melinda was away, so the first autopsy was done by one of the new assistant MEs. He's made a lot of mistakes."

Bob didn't react, and waited.

"This was a violent crime during or after sexual intercourse."

Bob said nothing.

"We have witness statements. One says, and I quote, 'He was a brute. He shouted at her all the time. Once I saw him grab her and shake her.' Here's another: 'He drank. Heavily. And he wanted her to drink. He was constantly pushing drinks on her.'"

Bob was taking notes. He kept his expression neutral.

"Ms. Yaeger's roommate states that she knew Ms. Yaeger was afraid of him, wanted to end the relationship. And, on the night of the murder, we have a statement from a neighbor who says she heard a serious argument on their doorstep. Ms. Yaeger wanted him to leave. Instead he pushed his way in."

"That's it? Hearsay? From a roommate? A young couple arguing and drinking? A nosy neighbor? That hardly adds up to murder."

"We'd be willing to accept a plea of manslaughter. Five years. He's a young guy. He'd still have a life in front of him when he got out."

"Yeah, as a convicted felon. Your case is weak, Billy. We both know it. It's got reasonable doubt written all over it. I'd say there isn't a chance in hell he'll accept that plea. I'll advise him not to take it."

"As you wish, counselor. Of course, we're still gathering evidence."

Bob put his notes in his briefcase and paused, changed his tone. "How have you been? How's Judy?"

Billy smiled. "Pregnant."

"That's wonderful. Congratulations. When is she due?"

"Three months. August. It's a boy." Lewis was smiling broadly. He and his wife already had a daughter.

"How's Marcus?" When Bob worked there, Lewis had been one of the friendlier ADAs.

"He's fine. Kenny is his graduate student."

"We thought that might be the case."

"See you in the morning."

"Nine o'clock. Courtroom C. Judge Esparza."

Bad news. Esparza was tough, especially on bail.

12

Bob wanted to talk to Kenny again, but it was now late and he knew he needed food and rest if he was going to be coherent in the morning.

On the short drive home, the exhaustion hit, and he tried to put together what he would tell the judge about bail. Young upstanding graduate student, no priors, weak prosecution case, release him on his own recognizance. Won't happen, but it's where he would start.

When he got home, Oscar did his usual happy dance at the door. Marcus and Jason were sitting at the dining room table, drinking tea, and Bob could smell tuna casserole. Marcus was a terrible cook, but a tuna casserole he could handle. Marcus got up to get it from the oven while Bob took off his tie and washed his hands and face.

As soon as Bob started eating, the phone in the kitchen rang; Marcus got up to answer it. It was Alex, Bob's brother in LA. He didn't make the usual small talk and asked to speak to Bob.

Marcus fetched Bob. "He sounds weird," he murmured as he handed Bob the phone.

Marcus heard Bob say "Oh, God" . . . "when?" . . . "okay." When he got back to the dining room, he looked stricken.

"Mom has cancer."

"What??"

Marcus stood up.

"Breast cancer. They think they caught it early. Surgery tomorrow."

"Tomorrow??"

"Well, they don't want to wait. Alex and Carol are flying out tonight on the red-eye." Carol was Alex's wife; they lived in Los Angeles. The senior Abramsons lived in Danbury, where the boys grew up.

"And Jay?" Marcus asked.

"They're leaving Jay with his friend George and his parents." Jay was their son, now ten years old, named after their father, Jake.

He hung up.

"They'll call as soon as they know anything." Bob was now pacing back and forth. "I've got that arraignment tomorrow. Maybe I can fly out in the afternoon. I should call now, it's late there."

Bob went to the bedroom to use the phone there; Marcus followed him. Jason cleared the table and loaded the dishwasher, but left Bob's plate out in case he wanted to finish; he hadn't had more than a few bites.

Bob dialed and Marcus heard him say "Dad." Then he mostly listened, saying little. Now it was Marcus doing the pacing. They were both close to Bob's parents, and Marcus could feel Bob's anxiety increasing with every moment.

"I just started a murder case," Bob told his father, also a lawyer. "The arraignment is in the morning. I'll fly out as soon as I can."

As he got off the phone, he started to cry. Marcus sat next to him on the bed and held him.

"What do they know so far?" Marcus asked, as gently as he could.

"It was a routine mammogram. She doesn't feel sick. They're pretty sure it's contained. They're doing a lumpectomy, assuming they don't see anything weird when they go in. Dad says they're both optimistic. Possibly chemo after the surgery."

"That's a good sign. The lumpectomy."

"Yeah, I guess."

"Come and finish dinner. You hardly ate anything."

Bob followed Marcus to the dining room, where he indifferently ate a few more bites. He turned to Jason.

"After the arraignment, have the office start demanding discovery. We need those witness statements. Start interviewing the witnesses. Apparently both Kenny and Cathy dated other people; we need to talk to those people. I should have the list from Kenny tomorrow after the arraignment. I don't know how complete it will be. We'll have to question Kenny again when I get back."

Jason nodded.

"Marcus, talk to people at Diversionary about Cathy. See what you can dig up."

Bob called Sarah, his secretary, at home, told her what was going on, and asked her to book him a flight for the next afternoon.

"Get some sleep," said Jason, getting up to leave. "You've had a hell of a day. We'll handle things here until you get back. Whatever you need."

Bob nodded and thanked him, and then collapsed on the living room sofa. Oscar came and rested his face on his knee.

Marcus didn't think he had ever seen Bob so upset. He tried to think of what to say.

"Breast cancer is survivable. It sounds like they caught it

early. Ruth is strong. It'll be okay."

"Hell of a time to start a murder trial," he said with a laugh. "Someday I'll forgive you for dragging me into this."

13

Bob tried to sleep but it was useless; he got up several times, drank herbal tea, then went back to bed, tossing and turning. Each time he went into the kitchen Oscar followed him and rested his face on Bob's knee as he sat at the kitchen table.

Oscar knew something was wrong. He always knew.

He finally got up at 6:00 and took a shower. Marcus got up, let Oscar outside, fed him, and made French toast, Bob's favorite breakfast, but he ate only a few bites. At 7:30, Sarah called with his flight information; his plane left at 1:00.

As he was packing a bag, Marcus brought Bob another cup of coffee.

"I was thinking," Marcus said. "If you're on a plane, you might miss the call from Alex. About the surgery. It's a long trip. Maybe it would be better to fly out tomorrow, when we know more?"

"No, I'll go today. I'll call as soon as I land at JFK."

Marcus knew Bob needed to be there. Practically from the moment they'd first met, Marcus could see how close Bob was to both his parents, so unlike his own family. It amazed him, the easiness of Ruth and Jake with a gay son, how quickly and warmly they welcomed Marcus into the family. They would introduce Marcus to everyone as their son-in-law as if it were the most natural thing in the world.

"Call me tonight," Marcus said, as he straightened Bob's tie and kissed him goodbye. Marcus could always tell Bob was upset when his tie wasn't straight.

Bob left for the arraignment and put himself on automatic pilot as soon as he mounted the courthouse steps.

The charge was first degree murder.

"How does the defendant plead?"

"Not guilty," Bob said. His voice was hoarse from lack of sleep.

There was a tangle over bail, as Bob expected. Kenny looked agitated and Bob wrote out "calm" on a legal pad, and underlined it.

He argued that Kenny should be released on his own recognizance, which, Bob knew, wouldn't happen. In the end bail was set at $2 million. The trial date was set for early October, a long way away, but Bob assumed the judge's docket must be crowded. He was relieved; he'd be able to spend time with his mother as she recovered, and they'd have time to dig into the case.

An attractive, very well dressed middle-aged couple was in the courtroom; Kenny's parents from Los Angeles. Kenny introduced them after the judge moved on to the next case and various people shuffled in and out of the courtroom. Bob shook hands with both of them, and noticed how firm his father's handshake was. Something about both of them made Bob uneasy. A whiff of pretension, maybe, or an air of artifice. Something odd. Something off.

Kenny was taken back to his cell; Bob walked his father through the bail process at the clerk's office. His mother said she'd wait outside. She looked vaguely familiar. He must have seen her on a TV show or in a film.

Not many people could just cough up $2 million, Bob

thought to himself, as his father wrote a check. He wondered where he made his money. The clerk, whom Bob knew, said they needed a cashier's check, but Bob talked him down. The clerk took a look at Joel Glick's $2,000 suit and figured the check was probably okay. Joel Glick, it turned out, was a major player in Los Angeles real estate.

Bob, with a document showing bail had been paid, collected Kenny and they joined his parents outside. It was another gorgeous San Diego morning. Kenny squinted at the sun.

Bob explained that he was leaving to be with his mother, who was having surgery in Connecticut.

Kenny's father was alarmed. "Should we find another lawyer?"

Bob said no, and Kenny agreed. "I'll be back soon. The trial is months away. For now, the only thing that needs to happen is for my investigator to collect witness statements and evidence. He's a former police detective, and I worked for the District Attorney. Your son is in good hands."

They all nodded, though Kenny's father looked skeptical.

"So what happens now?" Joel asked.

"There will be a preliminary hearing soon. Under California law, that has to happen within ten days, unless we ask for a postponement. We'd need at least a short postponement, given my family emergency. Which I'm sure we can get."

"What happens at that hearing?" Kenny asked.

"The judge hears some of the evidence from both sides and decides whether there is probable cause to bind you over for trial in Superior Court. Different judge. At this point, we don't have a lot of evidence proving your innocence, so I would attack the state's evidence and try to convince the judge there is not enough to go forward. It's a long shot. They've had a head start."

"Isn't it the case," Kenny's father asked, "that if we waive the hearing completely, they may offer a favorable plea deal?" It sounded to Bob like Joel had some knowledge about how these things worked, and Bob wondered how that had happened, and why he was bringing up a plea bargain.

"It's possible, yes."

"What would that look like?" Kenny asked.

"Well," Bob said, "we'd hope it was something like pleading guilty to manslaughter, with a short sentence."

"How short?" Kenny asked.

"It's difficult to say. Last night they were talking about five years."

"Five years??" Kenny nearly shouted.

"That was a first offer," Bob said, holding up his hand. "If they're starting from five, they could go down. Perhaps way down." Bob paused. "But there's another thing to consider."

"Go on," Joel said.

"As far as I can see, the state's case is weak. But this is a murder trial. We don't want to take chances. That means we need to do a lot of detective work. Investigate the state's witnesses, find ways of attacking their credibility. If possible, find the real criminal, or at least other suspects. All that takes time. Even if we ask for a delay, it won't be a long delay. Not with this judge."

Kenny looked at his father.

"Waive it. Do your work," Joel Glick said. "Find the killer."

Bob looked to Kenny. He nodded. "And I want my day in court," Kenny said. "With a jury. I didn't do this."

"Okay. If you're sure, we'll waive."

"We're sure," Joel Glick said. Bob realized that that was that.

Bob told Kenny it was extremely important that he not

say anything to anyone about the case. "Not a word. Not to your closest friend. Keep a low profile. Do not go to parties. Stay out of bars. Live like a monk. No dating."

Kenny did not look happy but said "okay."

As they walked toward the parking lot, Kenny's mother put her hand on Bob's arm. "I hope your mother will be fine." She smiled a beautiful smile. He remembered a friend from France once said "only Americans have teeth like that."

As his parents got into their BMW, Kenny hung back and gave Bob the lists he had asked for—sexual contacts.

It was a long list.

As he drove away, Bob had to wonder. Did Joel Glick push to waive the preliminary hearing because he thinks his son might be guilty, and he wants a plea deal? And was Kenny telegraphing to his parents, "I didn't do this, I'm not afraid, I want a jury?"

14

Bob drove to his office; he had time before his flight. Jason was waiting for him. Bob handed over the list.

"We need the toxicology report, and we need to talk to the ME who did the first autopsy. Exactly how much alcohol and what drugs were in her system? Why did the ME think that was the cause of death? Talk to Melinda if she's back, get her opinion, that will be crucial. And did Yaeger have any medical condition? Had she had sex with anyone besides Kenny in the days leading up to the murder? Start there."

Jason nodded. Sarah was taking notes.

They left Bob alone and he jotted down notes.

First autopsy v. second.

Sex with someone else?

No motive.

Rough sex not murder.

At 11:30 he left for the airport.

The flight left on time, and Bob dozed on the way to JFK. Flying across the country, coast to coast, always gave him a near-patriotic sense of its vastness that he found both comforting and unsettling. It was too big, he thought at times.

When he landed in New York City at 10:00 p.m. local time, he called the house. Carol, his sister-in-law, answered.

"It went well. They think they got it all. She'll need a couple of doses of chemo but she should be fine."

Bob felt like he could breathe for the first time in 24 hours. He rented a car, made it to Danbury when everyone but his brother was asleep.

They hugged.

"She's in good spirits," Alex said as they sat in the kitchen. "She was joking with the nurses. She'll be home soon. The chemo is outpatient."

Bob nodded.

"It's actually Dad I'm worried about. I've never seen him so shaken up. He's putting on a brave face but he's not himself."

Bob expected that.

"Carol can stay for a while. I have to get back soon. I imagine you do too."

Alex practiced corporate law in Los Angeles and was getting involved in local politics. He had been an early Clinton supporter and he was hoping there might be a job in the administration. There had been some preliminary interviews about something in the Justice Department, but no job offer had materialized, at least not yet.

"We'll figure out a schedule, we can take turns being here," Bob said. Then he had a thought. "When school is out, bring Jay. That'll make Mom happier than anything."

Alex hadn't thought of that; he nodded.

"And Marcus," Alex said. "He should come when he can. She loves him. I think she likes him more than she likes me at this point."

Bob laughed. "Oh, come on."

"No, I mean it. She's not happy that I backed Clinton, she thinks he's a fake. She calls him Slick Willie. Dad doesn't like him either but is less upset about it. They voted for Jerry Brown in the primary. Or Mom did. I'm not sure about Dad."

"Well, you've got to admit, Willie is off to a rocky start. I mean, Vince Foster's suicide. And living in San Diego, let me tell you about gays in the military—"

"Don't start. Sleep. We both need sleep."

Bob let the conversation drop and they both headed upstairs. Despite being on California time, Bob fell into a deep, child-like sleep.

15

In the morning Carol got up early and made eggs for everyone. Bob hugged her and his father and could see that Alex was right; his dad wasn't himself, although he was trying hard to sound upbeat.

Over breakfast Alex showed Bob and their father pictures of Jay, which he hoped would cheer him up. Jay cavorting in the ocean in Santa Monica, where Alex and Carol lived. Jay with Sophie, their golden retriever, who had given birth to Oscar. At the San Diego Zoo when they all visited Bob and Marcus. Jay was a happy child; anyone could see that from the pictures. Bob and Marcus both loved being his uncle.

Over second cups of coffee they talked about the next few days. Carol said she could stay.

"Don't be silly. Go home, take care of my grandson. Alex, you're in the middle of a big case, right?"

Alex nodded.

"And Bob, you've got a murder trial. We'll be fine. They'll let Ruth come home tomorrow, maybe even today. She'll need to rest, which will be hard for her, but we'll manage. We'll be fine."

No one wanted to argue. Bob said, "Well, we can take turns coming back over the summer, just to visit. Jay can come when school is out; that will make Mom happy."

Jake smiled. "Yes. It will."

Carol, who was already dressed, did the breakfast dishes while everyone else finished getting ready. Even though it was really early in California, Bob called Marcus, told him the news; he knew he would be worried.

"That's great. Give Mom my love."

They drove to the hospital in two cars, and, as they made their way to Ruth's room, they could hear her laughing with one of the nurses halfway down the hall. Bob loved his mother's laugh. Everyone kissed her, and she tried to hug them, but had to be careful because of the incision and the bandages. She looked tired but very much like herself.

"Go home," she said. "I'm fine."

"Mom," Alex said.

"Don't be silly. You have a big case. Both of you do," she said, looking at Bob. "And you need to take care of Jay," she added, looking at Alex. "The doctor's probably letting me go home later today, after some test results come back. I'll be fine."

"Mom . . ."

"Go home."

Carol intervened. "We'll stay tonight. You'll be tired. I'll cook dinner. We'll all leave tomorrow. You'll need to rest."

"That makes sense," Jake said, and that seemed to settle the matter.

"Okay, so, let's play Scrabble. One of the nurses brought me a set," Ruth said, laughing.

A good sign, Bob knew.

The doctor did let Ruth go home later in the day, and the first chemo session was scheduled for the following week. There would only be two.

When they all got home Ruth took a nap and Carol and Bob went grocery shopping, stocking up on everything. They cooked enough chicken to feed a family of twelve, thinking the leftovers would come in handy, and Carol made several cheesecakes. They loaded up on lunch meat.

While they ate dessert that night Ruth asked Bob about his new case.

"Murder. Looks like a sex crime. One of Marcus's graduate students."

They all looked at him.

He shrugged. "The prosecution case is weak. The kid had no motive, as far as I can see. And there are dueling autopsy reports. It should be easy," he said, trying to sound nonchalant.

Alex and Jake both knew a murder trial was never easy, but didn't say anything.

"Poor Marcus," Ruth said. "Is he upset?"

"Yes, somewhat. But he found the kid a really good lawyer."

Everyone chuckled.

After dinner they all made arrangements to fly home the next day, and Ruth went to bed early. The others settled in the den. There was a clap of thunder, and then it rained for about half an hour.

"That's one of the things I miss, living in San Diego," Bob said wistfully. "Rain."

In the morning he woke early and made French toast for everyone.

"This is Marcus's recipe. One of the few things he can cook without ruining it."

Ruth couldn't stop laughing at that.

They said their goodbyes after breakfast, and Ruth went back to bed. With Jake, they made a tentative schedule for coming back to visit.

Bob took a long nap on the plane. Mercifully, the seat next to him was empty.

Marcus picked him up at the airport when he landed at 3:00 o'clock California time. Oscar was in the back seat and went delirious when he saw Bob, and kept trying to climb into the front to be with him. Marcus finally stopped the car and Bob got into the back seat and Oscar calmed down. He wouldn't leave Bob's side for the rest of the day, and that night, instead of sleeping in his doggy bed, he slept on the floor on Bob's side of the bed.

16

The next morning Bob got up early, as usual, and took Oscar for a long walk. He showered and dressed and called Jason and Sarah at home, told them to meet him at the office at noon. He had to clear away a few other things on his desk before diving into Kenny Glick's case. He liked giving both of them the morning or afternoon off whenever he could; they both worked hard, often long past normal working hours or on weekends. He didn't know how he would have managed without them. At the moment, he was between law clerks, not an ideal situation with a murder trial looming.

"Anything yet?" he asked Jason on the phone.

"Not much. Melinda's father is definitely dying. In Russia. She's going to be away for a while. I interviewed her assistant ME, who did the first autopsy. He swears the bruising on Yaeger wasn't there when he examined her. He says those kinds of bruises can take a couple of days to show. A copy of his report is on your desk."

"Good. Talk to a few doctors, see if what he says about the bruising is likely."

"Copy that. How's your mother?"

"She's okay. They say she'll be fine."

"I'm glad. See you later."

Over breakfast, Bob asked Marcus if he had had a chance to talk to anyone at Diversionary about Cathy Yaeger.

"Not yet. I was planning see some of them today. They've been rehearsing *Street Theater* and Cathy had been in the cast, which is large. They have a rehearsal late this afternoon. I'll go then. Some of them must have known Cathy well, I'd guess. They'd been in previous shows together."

Street Theater, Bob knew, was a play about Stonewall; he had read the script along with Marcus when the theater was considering it. This summer would be the twenty-fifth anniversary of the uprising that had sparked the modern gay rights movement. It would be the second play performed in Diversionary's newly opened theater space; Marcus, a board member, had been deeply involved in raising money to get the job done.

The space, on the second floor of a small office complex, had cost over $100,000 to renovate and turn into a theater. Raising the money was a slog, and a major accomplishment. Before it opened, the group had performed everywhere from a dilapidated community center to a junior high school auditorium. In those early years Marcus had done everything from helping build sets to selling drinks at intermission. He loved the theater and he was determined to make it prosper, which it had. It took his mind off his academic career.

After giving Oscar his morning quota of scratches and a belly rub, they both left for work.

17

At the office Bob cleared away paper work from recently closed cases, then looked at the ME report.

Cathy Yaeger had Demerol and alcohol in her system. A lot of alcohol. Marcus was surprised. Demerol was a powerful opiate prescribed for pain and sometimes for sleep, and combining it with alcohol, Bob knew, could be dangerous. The ME concluded that the combination stopped her heart.

The Demerol raised a red flag. Had it been prescribed? For what? Did Yaeger have a chronic pain condition of some kind? Seemed unlikely for someone her age, but they needed to find out.

Jason arrived a few minutes before noon, followed by Sarah, who brought in sandwiches and cups of coffee for lunch; that was the usual routine when they met at lunchtime.

"I talked to a couple of medical contacts," Jason said, munching on his roast beef. "They said yes, bruises can take twenty-four to seventy-two hours to appear, although they were just guessing; they need to see the actual photos."

Bob nodded.

Jason added that he had also talked to some of the women Kenny had dated, and heard nothing suspicious.

Sarah said she had been in touch with Billy Lewis's office and they would have copies of the photos and witness statements on Monday. It was Friday. Given the quick trip East and worry about his mother, Bob barely knew what day it was.

"Cathy Yaeger had Demerol in her system," Bob said. "A high dose, apparently. That's unusual for someone her age. First up, who prescribed it, and for what?"

"The ME agreed it was suspicious. Off the record," Jason said.

"Who is this assistant ME?"

"Robert Goldstein. UCSD Med School. Internship and residency there in pathology. Harvard undergrad."

"Well, we shouldn't hold that against him." Bob had been an undergraduate at Brown and applied to Harvard but didn't get in. He did, though, go to Harvard Law, and Marcus had been an assistant professor there when they met. They both found the place snobbish to a ridiculous degree and were happy to get away from it. The Center of Western Culture, some called it, without a trace of irony.

Jason guffawed.

"Seriously, though," Bob said. "Great credentials. Doesn't mean he didn't mess up, although Melinda is so meticulous, it's hard to imagine she'd hire a screw-up. See if you can find out if he's made any mistakes on other cases. Is there any way to reach Melinda?"

"We can try," Jason said, "But it won't be easy. Apparently her father lives in a remote area without a phone."

"I wonder how Melinda got herself here in the first place," Bob said. Sarah said she'd work on finding a way to reach her. "Maybe a telegram, asking her to call."

"Good. Also, make sure the other autopsy report is in the material the DA turns over, the one done by the family."

Sarah nodded.

"We need to find out everything we can about Cathy Yaeger. And about Kenny Glick. Glick admits they did not have an exclusive relationship. Who else were they seeing? From what Billy Lewis told me, it sounds like their relationship was volatile, maybe even slightly violent. We need to know more. A lot more."

Bob took a bite of his tuna fish. The taste of the tuna reminded him of something.

"What about semen samples?"

"There was a match to Glick, the ME said. He gave a voluntary cheek swab when the police first questioned him."

Marcus wondered why Glick hadn't mentioned that. "Not a surprise, he admitted they had sex that night. But was there someone else's semen as well?"

"No. But of course if she had showered, or if someone used a condom . . ."

"Right. She might have had sex with someone else the previous night, or the night before, and there would be no trace. Glick says he left for the gym that morning at 6 a.m. Someone else could have come in and done the murder. Did any of her neighbors see anyone? Did the police fingerprint the place? And did anyone see Glick at the gym?"

Both Sarah and Jason were writing.

"There should be crime scene photos. Was there any sign

of a struggle? Show them to Glick, ask him if anything looks out of place. The slightest change could matter. Someone could have gone to her apartment after Glick left at six. Did the ME say anything about time of death?"

"He said it was very hard to pin down, given everything in her system."

"That doesn't help. We need everything we can find about Yaeger's background."

"On it," Jason said.

"I think that's it."

It was now 1:30, and Bob was feeling his jet lag. "Do a little today and then take the rest of the day off. We'll kick into high gear next week, when we get the DA file. The trial isn't until October. We have time."

Sarah collected the sandwich wrappers and they both left Bob alone.

"Jason, you have mustard on your shirt," Sarah said with a smirk.

Bob called Marcus, who was in his campus office.

"Hey. It's your favorite lawyer. What time are you going to Diversionary?"

"Around five."

"I'll meet you there."

"Maybe you shouldn't? I mean, they might talk more freely if it's just me."

"Good point. But I need to ask questions. I'll be charming."

Marcus laughed.

Bob hung up, made some notes about the case. Then, on an impulse, he called a doctor friend, who was between patients and had a minute to talk.

"So off the record," Bob said, "tell me. Can Demerol combined with alcohol kill someone? A young woman?"

"How much of each?"

Bob read Jeff the numbers.

"That's a lot. Of both. Could be a lethal combination. No question."

"Is Demerol available on the street? Without a prescription?"

"Everything is available on the street around here. Remember how close we are to Mexico. And, if it was bought on the street, it could have been laced with something else, or impure."

Bob hadn't thought of that.

"Thanks Jeff, I owe you one."

"How's Marcus?"

"Well, you know, he's over 40 now. I may have to trade him in for a newer model."

Jeff laughed. "Nah, older is better. Besides, you're the most solid couple we know."

Bob smiled to himself. It was true. Even after ten years, they were as happy together as when they first met, even if they had sex a little less frequently.

"Seriously, though, is he okay?" Jeff asked. "Turning 40 can trigger . . . all sorts of things."

"He seems fine, actually. A little stuck on his work project but that's nothing new."

"Make sure he has an annual physical. We should all have dinner soon." Jeff's partner Don was a real estate agent.

"Definitely."

Bob then dialed Danbury. His mother picked up on the first ring.

"Hey. How do you feel?"

"I'm fine sweetheart, really. The incision hurts a bit, but my energy is coming back. The doctor called and said the pathology report was fine. The neighbors keep dropping off food. We should be feeding the poor."

Bob laughed. "Good. When is the first chemo?"

"Next Wednesday. Don't worry. It will be fine."

"I'm sure it will be. But chemo can knock you out. Take it easy. No gardening."

Ruth laughed. "No, I'm just baking. Your father is watching over me like a hawk. It reminds me of when Alex was born. Your father kept going to the crib to make sure he was still breathing."

Bob laughed.

"Of course, by the time you arrived, we were blasé. Hardly noticed you."

"Well, that explains a lot."

"Have a good weekend, sweetheart. Give my love to Marcus."

"Will do. Rest."

"I'll send you some poppy seed cake."

18

After clearing away more paperwork, Bob told Sarah and Jason to go home. He had a little time to kill before meeting Marcus, so he drove out to the Ocean Beach pier and walked all the way to the end. It was a beautiful day, if a bit overcast, and the ocean was churning, which meant the surfers were out in full force. At the end of the pier you could watch them catch the back of the wave and glide to shore.

It was hypnotic, and Bob felt the week's stress leaching out of his body. He loved the smell and sound of the ocean, the gulls, the funky tie-dyed T-shirts people wore in that neighborhood, keeping the 1960s alive. The Pacific was a wild ocean compared to the Atlantic, the only ocean he had known as a child and young adult on the East coast.

At 4:30 he left to meet Marcus at Diversionary in University Heights, the neighborhood tucked between Hillcrest and Normal Heights. The new theater space was up a long flight of outside stairs, with a balcony where audience members congregated during intermissions. Inside, the theater held 104 red seats that Marcus and another board member had somehow procured from a strange man who kept a variety of theater paraphernalia in his garage. The seats were arranged in a semicircle around the stage. It was an intimate space but not tiny. The first play in the new space had opened a few months before, in February, and Marcus and other board members and the crew were still painting walls at 5:00 on opening night. But the performance was on time, and flawless.

He found Marcus inside talking to a few young actors from the upcoming play. Like some of Marcus's students, a few of them were wearing plaid flannel shirts and torn jeans. For reasons Bob couldn't fathom, some kids in their late teens and twenties wanted to look like they lived in Seattle rather than in warm Southern California.

"Most of you know my other half, Bob," he said, and everyone nodded. "He's looking into Cathy Yaeger's murder."

At the mention of Cathy's name, their expressions changed; two of them looked away. Just then Andy Rich, the play's director, came in from backstage, holding a pile of scripts. Marcus got up to speak to him, and signaled Bob to come closer.

"Andy, you know Bob." They smiled-nodded to each other. "Could we have a quick word outside?"

They went out to the balcony.

"Andy, Bob has been hired to defend Kenny Glick."

"I see."

Bob asked Andy if he had ever met him.

"Yes, a few times, briefly, at parties, cast parties, that sort of thing. He and Cathy were together a lot."

"Did you get a sense of their relationship? It's hard to talk about this, I know."

"Well," Andy said, choosing his words carefully. "I think their relationship was tempestuous."

"How do you mean?"

"A lot of shouting. Both of them. Storming out of the room. That sort of thing. And they both drank. A lot. At rehearsals Cathy was sometimes really out of it, couldn't focus, and I'd smell liquor on her breath. Most of the time, though, she was a terrific young actress, very focused. She definitely had a future. But..."

"But?"

"She was high-strung. A lot of actors are, but it was extreme in her case. At least, that's how it seemed to me."

"Did you ever see anything you'd call violent between Cathy and Ken?"

"Well I saw Cathy slap Ken hard, once, at a party. Then Ken grabbed her by the shoulders and said something to her, I don't know what, and she softened. She smiled. They both did. I got the sense they were like that when they were together."

"I see. Ever see anything else like that slap?"

He thought for a moment. "Not that I can remember."

"Thanks, that's helpful. If it's all right with you, I'd like to talk to members of your cast who knew them, or who knew Cathy."

"You can ask them, sure."

"Thanks. Will you announce what's happening? I'll talk

to them one-on-one out here. Just send out anyone who is willing to talk."

Marcus asked Bob if he wanted him to stay.

"No, Pinky, probably better if I talk to them alone."

Marcus nodded. "See you at home. I'll cook something."

Bob winced.

19

What Bob heard from the five or six actors who came out to talk mostly matched what Andy had told him. Volatile relationship. Lots of shouting. Lots of drinking. Maybe some drugs, coke or weed. Lots of fights and lots of making up. But one young woman provided some startling information.

Her name was Beth, and she said she and Cathy had been close, had shared an apartment for a while. Even when no longer roommates, they saw each other often, she said, and had been in several plays together.

"Cathy was a method actor, and serious about it, and she wanted every kind of experience in life."

"What do you mean by 'method'?"

"Method acting. The basic idea is that the actor analyzes each scene for their character's motivation and emotion, and then, when they play the scene, they call to mind something from their own life that matches that as closely as possible. That way, when it works, your tone of voice, your body language and facial expression will be real. It's difficult. It takes a lot of practice and concentration."

"I see." Bob had heard the term "method" applied to

actors like Brando, but never knew what it meant.

"And Cathy took it really seriously. I think that's part of what attracted her to Ken. He took her places she wouldn't have gone otherwise. So to speak."

"Can you say more?"

Beth hesitated.

"I know," Bob said, trying to sound like a therapist, "this is hard to talk about. But you can really help Cathy by telling me what you know."

Bob always hated using that line, it was such a cliché, but it sometimes worked.

"Well, Cathy said they explored some unusual sexual scenes. Sometimes three-ways, that kind of thing. Some kink. Ken was adventurous that way. And Cathy once said he encouraged her to be with as many guys as possible."

Bob tried to hide his surprise.

"Did she do all that willingly?"

"Yes. At first it bothered her, but after a while I think she enjoyed it. Grist for the mill, she called it. Experiences for her acting."

"And she used the word 'kink'?"

"Yeah, she did."

"Can you say more about what she meant?"

"She didn't get graphic. But I did once see her wearing a leather collar. She called it a fashion accessory and laughed, but I think it was more than that."

"I see. Had you seen her recently?"

"Not really, no. We hadn't gotten together for a month or so, except here when rehearsals started."

"But you were good friends. And she confided in you?"

"Yes, we were good friends." Beth started to tear up.

"How well did you know Kenny?"

"Not real well, but I knew him. I think when they weren't fighting, they cared about each other."

"Thank you for being so honest. I really appreciate it. Did you know any of the other men she saw? Or did she tell you about them?"

"Well, I know that one was a professor at UCSD. That's all I know about him."

Again Bob tried to hide his surprise.

"Anyone else?"

"Someone who lived at the beach here in town. Some guys in LA. And a rich guy in Palm Springs. An actor who had a house there. Cathy said he had been in some movies. She didn't tell me who, or say any more. But she was there several times, I know that. I think she hoped he could help her career."

Just then Andy came out and said they needed Beth in the next scene.

"This is very helpful. Thanks. Thanks for being so honest."

Beth tried to smile and went back to rehearsal.

20

Bob talked to a couple more of the young actors, who had nothing new to add, and then stuck his head in to the theater, thanked everyone.

He left some business cards at the edge of the stage. "If any of you think of anything else, please give me a call."

Kinky sex. He hadn't expected that. And how many young men encouraged their girlfriends to sleep around? Clearly this was a different Kenny from the one Marcus knew.

And Kenny had not come clean; that bothered him. He had

said something about "horsing around." That's not what this sounded like. And, based on what Andy had said, they clearly drank more than an occasional glass of wine with dinner.

He debated how much he would tell Marcus. He didn't want Marcus to be upset, but he didn't see how to keep this from him. Bob knew there would be conversations with Jason, either at the house or over the phone, that Marcus would overhear; that had happened often enough in various earlier cases. And maybe Marcus could help him track down the UCSD professor who might now be a suspect.

And he trusted Marcus. He had never been indiscreet about Bob's work. Yes, he would tell him. Maybe hearing Beth's story would jog Marcus's memory about something; that happened sometimes in cases like this. Criminal cases were sometimes like a group of people watching a cook slowly peel an onion. Sometimes, as each layer was peeled away, someone remembered something they had forgotten, or didn't think was relevant.

When he got home, Oscar greeted him wildly just as Marcus was shouting "God damn it" in the kitchen.

"I ruined another chicken," Marcus called out.

"But Pinky, you tried." Bob hugged him from behind. The chicken did in fact look like a charred mess. "We'll order in."

21

Over take-out Italian food, Bob gave Marcus the gist of what he had heard.

"Jesus. I would not have expected that. Any of it. Do you think she was telling the truth?"

"I can't be sure, you never know with a witness, especially when they're not under oath, but yes, that was my sense."

Marcus nodded.

"Did you ever pick up any vibe like that from Kenny?"

Marcus thought for a moment. "No, not from Kenny. But . . ."

"But?"

"But I get the general sense that a lot of students these days treat sex a lot more casually than we did. They don't see it as a big deal, they see it as play. Recreation. A game."

"Like pre-AIDS gay men."

"Yeah, I hadn't thought of that, but yes."

They both were quiet for a moment, lost in thought.

"So you'll need to confront Kenny with this, right?" Marcus asked.

"Right. In fact I'll call him tonight, try to meet with him over the weekend."

They did the dishes and then Bob left a message at Kenny's number; Kenny called back as Bob and Marcus were watching a video of *Chinatown*, one of their favorite films. They had first seen the film in Boston but didn't appreciate it fully until they moved to San Diego, the depiction of the desperation for water as giant cities grew up in a dessert. And they both thought Faye Dunaway was amazing.

Bob arranged to meet Kenny the next afternoon at his office.

"Could we meet somewhere else?" Kenny asked. "Over coffee, or somewhere like that?"

"No," Bob said, "we need to meet where no one can overhear us."

In the morning Bob and Marcus slept late, as they usually did on weekends, and finally got up when Oscar made a fuss, as he always did when one of them didn't get up early enough to feed him and let him outside. He would lay his face down on one side of the bed and give them his most pathetic look, and if that didn't work, he would start vocalizing. He never barked but had a litany of sounds for every occasion.

"Yes, your majesty," Marcus said as he got out of bed.

Bob made pancakes, which they ate outside while they read the local papers. Afterward, Marcus went to his study to do some work and Bob did some weeding in the yard; he then went inside to prepare boeuf bourguignon for dinner, leaving Marcus strict instructions on how to cook it.

"Two-and-a-half hours. Don't forget. Set the timer. Don't let it burn."

"Yes, sir."

Bob dressed and drove to the office, where Kenny was waiting for him outside. He tried to get himself in the right frame of mind to elicit information without sounding upset or angry. Or suspicious.

22

Bob offered Kenny a soft drink from the little fridge in his inner office. They both took a ginger ale.

"Ken, you know that anything we discuss is completely confidential. I cannot divulge anything you say to anyone unless you say you're about to commit a crime."

Kenny nodded.

"And you understand I need a full picture of your relationship with Cathy?"

Kenny nodded again, but began to look nervous.

"In a case like this, I need to understand the life of the deceased, if for no other reason than to see if there are any suspects other than my client. So I started by talking to some people who knew Cathy at Diversionary."

Kenny shifted in his seat.

"Her friend Beth was one of them. You knew her, right?"

Kenny nodded.

"She says you encouraged Cathy to explore some kinky sexual scenes. With a lot of different people."

"Do we really have to talk about this? I mean, aren't we entitled to privacy?"

"Ken, you're going to be on trial for murder. We can't be squeamish about any of this. Too much is at stake. I'm not here to judge your sex life."

That wasn't entirely true, Bob acknowledged to himself, but maybe it would help to say it.

Kenny nodded.

"And keep in mind, anything we discover, the police certainly can."

"Okay. I get it."

"Did you encourage Cathy to explore kinkier sex? To be with other men? Did you engage in group sex?"

Kenny stood up and went to the window, with his back to Bob. A long moment passed.

"Yes."

"Yes to all three?"

"Yes to all three."

"Okay."

"You've got to understand," Kenny said, as he returned to his chair, "Cathy was into it. She thought it would help her acting. She enjoyed it."

"Beth said that too. Did any of the experiences involve

violence? Something that could have left those bruises on her? You remember the photos from the second autopsy. The prosecution is going to rely heavily on those photos."

"You have to understand. Everything was consensual."

"I can believe that." Bob was thinking of what Marcus had said about his students. "But is it possible something got out of hand? How rough could things get?"

"A little rough. Hard . . ." Kenny groped for the right word, "hard penetration. And maybe some hands around the neck, that sort of thing."

That was important.

"Were you always present for these scenes?"

"No. No! Sometimes yes, but Cathy saw people on her own." He looked down. "We both did."

"Can you be more specific about these scenes?"

"Some involved leather, costumes. Sometimes Cathy liked to be play dominant, a dominatrix."

"Go on."

"Sometimes group things. Three, four, maybe five."

"Whips? Choking?"

Kenny looked down.

"Yes, sometimes. But not hard. It was all play. Honest."

Bob chose his words carefully. "Would it be fair to say you brought Cathy into this world?"

Kenny looked at the painting on the wall, a reproduction of the Kandinsky they had sold. "Yes."

Bob was impressed with his matter-of-factness. A guilty man would deny it, or waffle.

"Do you know if Cathy was with anyone in the day or two before she was found dead?"

"I don't know."

"Is it possible?"

"Yes." Kenny looked away, and sounded slightly angry.

"And the night you spent with her, before she died, were you rough in any way?"

"No. Definitely not."

Bob was taking notes.

"The police say they have a report from a neighbor who saw you two arguing on the threshold to her apartment that night."

Kenny thought for a moment. "I don't remember. It's possible. We did have a lot of arguments. I guess we both had pretty bad tempers." He let out another of his little laughs.

"And you don't remember if you argued that night, or what it might have been about?"

"No. Like I said before, we had drinks first. We might have both been feeling the alcohol. I don't know. It was just an ordinary night."

Bob realized he needed to stop; Kenny was getting upset. He was at a point he recognized from experience, the point where a client or a witness stops telling the truth, or the whole truth.

"Okay. Just a few more questions."

Kenny nodded and took a long drink of his ginger ale.

"Beth said Cathy was seeing a professor at UCSD. Do you know who?"

"Tom Shannon. He's a scientist of some sort."

"Did you ever meet him?"

"No."

"And Beth mentioned some men in LA and Palm Springs. I need names if you have them."

Kenny got up and looked out the window again.

"Richard Cartwright."

"The actor?"

"Yeah."

Bob tried not to sound surprised.

"Any other names you can give me?"

"Alex Johnson. A rich guy in LA."

The name rang a bell but Bob couldn't place him.

"Okay. Thanks. This is helpful." Bob knew he needed to stop there. "At the beginning of the week the prosecution will turn over witness statements and other evidence they claim to have. We'll need to meet again to go over that material."

"Okay."

"One more thing. The police had asked you for a DNA sample?"

"Yes."

"I need to hear things like that. And from now on, you say not a word to the police, or anyone else, unless I'm present. Did they search your apartment?"

"Yes."

"I should have been there."

"Okay. Sorry." He got up and headed to the door. He turned around. "You've got to understand something. I loved her. I wouldn't have hurt her. I know we were kinda wild, but that doesn't mean I killed her."

"I know. Try not to worry. I'll be in touch at the beginning of the week."

23

After he was gone, Bob let out a long breath. The fact that they both had tempers wouldn't play well with a jury. Nor would the kinky sex. Especially the kinky sex. But there was now a group of possible suspects. They would have to be interviewed, that is, if they could be found. Jason could screen many of them for alibis. Could any of them have been with Cathy in the day or two before she died? Could there have been a jealous partner who wanted more than she was willing to give? Bob had seen that before.

Lots of grounds here for reasonable doubt.

He wondered if Kenny was telling the truth about the argument that night. He needed to see the witness statement from Cathy's neighbor.

Bob checked his watch. It was now 4:30. He called Marcus.

"Don't worry, I just put it in the oven. I didn't even spill it. It will be ready at seven."

Bob chuckled. Then he called Jason, filled him in, gave him the names Kenny had given him.

"Monday morning, see what you can find out about any of them."

"I know one thing now. Alex Johnson is married to Maude Strauss Cunningham. Her second husband. Or maybe third."

"Oh. My. God."

Maude was the matriarch of one of the richest families in California. Bob had run across her son James several years before when he worked in the DA's office. James was, as one of the cops on that case said, a piece of work.

"Are you sure?"

"Positive."

"How old is Johnson?"

"Sixty-ish."

"What does he do?"

"As little as possible. He won the lottery. He married a Cunningham."

Bob laughed. "Monday morning, see if he has any kind

of record, or if your contacts here or in LA have ever run across him."

"Will do."

"This case is getting more interesting."

"Yeah. Headline stuff."

Kenny's arrest had already been featured prominently in the local press. Bob hated that kind of publicity but he had to admit, it was good for business.

"I smell movie rights," Jason joked.

"Mini-series. Prestige television is where the action is these days."

They both laughed.

"Did he do it? I mean Glick."

"I don't think so. But he admits, he has a temper. There's the witness from that night. We need to see that statement. Interview that witness. And then there are those photos from the second autopsy. Devastating. We need to talk to the first ME and Melinda."

"Sarah is working on it. I think she sent a telegram."

"Okay good. See you Monday."

Another Cunningham, Bob thought. *Just what I need.*

24

The beef was, in fact, ready at 7:00 and tasted great. They both ate too much. Oscar sat at the edge of the table, lured by the smell of meat, hoping for a scrap, but they had decided never to feed him from the table. He was a devil when it came to food; he had once stolen a hamburger off the kitchen counter when Bob briefly left the room.

They went to bed early.

Sunday morning was overcast and drizzly, the beginning of what the natives called June gloom, even though it often started in May. They loafed around the house, reading the Sunday *New York Times* and the local papers. That evening they had tickets to see *The Cherry Orchard* at the La Jolla Playhouse, starring Lynn Redgrave. Marcus had resisted the idea when Bob suggested they get tickets.

"It's Chekhov. His plays are about boredom. Nothing even happens."

Bob laughed. "It's a Redgrave. Live. And his best play. We're going."

Redgrave was, in fact, magnificent. She possessed every moment on stage.

"Wow," Marcus said in the car going home. "I'm glad you made me go to that. That was an incredible performance. I've never seen anything like it."

On Monday morning Sarah called as Bob was dressing to say she was picking up the discovery material from the DA on her way to the office. Then Jason called to say he had spoken briefly to Gus Bobbitt, one of the detectives who arrested Kenny, who said, off the record, that there was no evidence that Cathy Yaeger had ever been prescribed Demerol.

That was troubling. Either she was buying it on the street, or someone gave it to her. The prosecution would say that someone was Glick.

Jason also said he had checked with a couple of doctors, both of whom agreed the Demerol plus alcohol could have killed Yaeger. And so far, nothing unusual from Kenny or Cathy's sexual contacts. "Though," Jason added, "who knows if they're telling the truth."

Bob got to the office early; Sarah arrived a few minutes

later and handed him a packet of material from the DA.

The witness who called Glick a "brute" and saw him "shake" Cathy was Maureen Freeman, a student at UCSD. She testified that she saw this happen at a party, although she could not remember the location or the date of the party, or who else was present.

Her statement was vague, and the lack of detail could be helpful to the defense.

The witness who testified that Kenny drank heavily and "wanted" Cathy to drink was Jane Masters, another UCSD undergraduate. She also was vague about dates and location.

Again, a lack of detail.

Cathy Yaeger's roommate was named Susan Tierney. She testified that Cathy was "afraid" of Kenny and wanted to end the relationship. She was vague about any specific conversation in which Cathy revealed this to her.

That could be damning testimony, but her vagueness probably meant Bob could create doubts about her accuracy.

The most damaging statement was from Cathy Yaeger's neighbor, Rebecca Morrison, who was 73 years old. She testified she heard and saw Cathy and Kenny arguing and shouting in front of the door to Cathy's apartment on the night of the murder, and that Kenny "pushed his way in."

After reading the statements, Bob got up and fetched a cup of coffee, thinking that if this was all they had, it was not a strong case. Arguing and drinking does not prove murder beyond a reasonable doubt.

Bob called Kenny and left a message on his machine, asking him to come to the office at 3:00.

Sarah buzzed Bob to say Melinda Ivanov was on the line.

"Melinda, thanks so much for calling. How is your father?" The phone connection was terrible.

"Not well. He's dying. Slowly. My mother died a long time ago, and my brother was killed in the army. Afghanistan. I'm all he has left."

"I'm so sorry. And I'm sorry to bother you with this, but it's a murder case."

"I understand."

Bob gave her the facts.

"Do you trust this new ME, Goldstein?"

"Yes. Absolutely. He's not been wrong so far. He worked for the coroner in Boston for two years before coming here, with a stellar record. He moved here because his wife got a job here."

That contradicted what Bob had been told by Billy Lewis, which again suggested the police were trying to force Kenny into a plea bargain.

Bob then described the bruises on Yaeger's body from the second autopsy.

"Could those bruises have taken time to appear?"

"Yes, especially if this was light bruising. Of course I'd need to see the actual photos."

He then asked her if alcohol and Demerol could be the cause of death, and she confirmed that it could. And she confirmed that she had seen cases of Demerol bought on the street, impure or laced with other substances, even baby powder.

"Thank you Melinda, this is incredibly helpful."

"You're welcome. What is the trial date?"

"Not until October."

"I'll be back by then. He can't last much longer."

25

Bob felt better about the case when he got off the phone, although there were still troubling details, especially the Demerol. Where did it come from? Why was she taking it?

He could hear Jason talking to Sarah, and asked them both to come in. He quickly summarized what was in the witness statements and what Melinda had said.

"We need to set up interviews with the witnesses. Sarah, they're all women, you make initial contact with them."

Sarah nodded.

"Jason, you work on setting up interviews with the rest of the men Cathy has been with, at least the ones we know about so far. Have you found anything on any of them?"

"Shannon, Cartwright, and Johnson all have clean records. Johnson once faced a civil suit about some investments, but he was not found liable and the records of the case were sealed. That's it." It was unusual for the record in a civil case to be sealed, Bob knew, but then the Cunninghams had more pull than any family in California. They controlled most of the newspapers in the state.

Jason asked whether there was a police report about the search of Cathy's apartment and Glick's.

"Yes." Bob handed both reports to Jason. He looked them over.

"Nothing about Demerol, or anything else suspicious. No signs of a struggle at Yaeger's apartment. Nothing."

"Isn't this an awfully weak case?" Sarah asked.

"It is, unless they're holding something back. And I wouldn't put that past them. Or maybe they think they'll find more witnesses or more evidence. So far, there's enough to cast suspicion on Kenny, but suspicion doesn't mean twelve jurors are going to vote to convict on a murder charge."

"How is Melinda?" Sarah asked.

"Her father is definitely dying. She didn't say much more than that."

"We'll get going on setting up those interviews."

"Right, thanks. Sarah, if you can, track down the women."

She nodded. "Don't forget," she added, "you have those interviews with clerk applicants. One at eleven and one at one o'clock."

Bob nodded. He had in fact completely forgotten.

The eleven o'clock interviewee was a Stanford Law graduate who wore a fancy suit and gave the impression he knew he'd be slumming by taking this job. But the afternoon candidate was promising. Anna Mendoza had grown up in San Diego and just finished law school at Berkeley. She wanted to undertake criminal defense work. She was personable and smart and had a strong academic record. She'd passed the state bar. Bob said he'd check her references and get back to her as soon as he could. And she was quite beautiful. Bob hated the fact, but appearances mattered, especially to juries.

At 3:00 Kenny arrived.

Bob told him about the witness statements and asked for his take. He had only a vague recollection of the UCSD undergraduates, he said. He also claimed he had no knowledge of Cathy's relationship with the three men she had been with. She had mentioned Shannon's name, he said, but that was all.

"And Susan Tierney? Cathy's roommate?"

"Yes, I knew her. Don't worry. She won't be a convincing witness."

"How do you mean?"

Kenny shifted in his chair. He was thinking.

"I shouldn't explain," he finally said. "At least not yet. But trust me. If the prosecution calls her, they'll be sorry. I watch *Law & Order*. And old *Perry Mason* episodes."

Bob sighed. The digital generation. He wanted to know more, but he was tired, and he still needed to do some work on another case before going home.

He let it go.

26

The next day, a Tuesday, Bob spent working on another case, a DUI. In the morning he met with his client, a Marine, and convinced him to plead guilty—it was a first offense, no jail time—and in the afternoon they went to court to plead.

Late in the day, Jason told him they had an interview with Tom Shannon, one of Cathy's trysts, the following morning at 11:00 on the UCSD campus.

Bob called Marcus, who was in his campus office.

"Can you make a few discreet inquiries about Tom Shannon? What kind of guy is he, is he married, that sort of thing?"

"I can try, but I don't know many people in the sciences. Most of them have their labs, socialize with each other . . . that kind of thing."

"Well whatever you can find."

"Okay, Pinky. I'll try."

That night over Thai take-out Marcus reported in.

"I talked to two people. Both are in Biology, but that

department is so huge it's like its own little university. I told them I was about to be on a committee this guy was chairing, which would never happen, but whatever. He's described as young and brilliant. Does research on toxins and their impact on the human brain. Unmarried."

"Hm. Thanks. Unmarried is interesting. How old is he?"

"Early thirties."

As they were cleaning up after dinner, Sarah called; they had an interview with Rebecca Morrison, Cathy's neighbor, at 3:00 the next afternoon.

After dinner Marcus had papers to grade and Bob took Oscar for a long walk. It was a beautiful evening and lots of people were out and about, and Oscar, as usual, greeted everyone with delirious joy.

27

The next morning Jason drove them to the UCSD campus to meet Shannon. His lab was in a huge, ugly building made of gray cinder blocks, one of the many new, ugly science buildings that had been built quickly and cheaply on campus over the last few years. They informed a secretary why they were there, and she showed them into Shannon's sparsely furnished office a few doors down from his lab.

Shannon entered wearing a white lab coat.

"Gentlemen. I'm Tom Shannon." He shook hands with both of them. He was a handsome man, blond hair, tall, and Bob guessed him to be around thirty-five. "What can I do for you?"

"We've been retained by Kenneth Glick, who is accused

of the murder of Catherine Yaeger. We're looking into all aspects of the case," Bob said.

At the mention of Cathy's name, Shannon's expression changed from friendly to worried.

"I see. Please go on."

"We've been told by a close friend of hers that you may have known her."

"Yes, I did."

"I'm sorry to pry, and we're not here to judge, but was your relationship intimate?"

"Yes." Shannon sounded straightforward, matter of fact.

"How did you meet?"

"We ran into each other at the Grove. It was crowded that day and I was sitting at one of the tables, and she asked if she could join me. There was nowhere else to sit. So we got to talking."

The Grove, Bob knew, was an outdoor café on campus among a large clump of eucalyptus trees, which grew everywhere on campus. It was a lovely spot.

"And how often did you see each other?"

"Perhaps once a week for a few months." Shannon took a swig of water from a plastic bottle on his desk. "She was a lovely person. I was very sorry to hear about what had happened to her."

"Do you recall when was the last time you were together?"

Shannon thought for a moment. "It was right after Easter. So that would have been the first week of April."

"And how would you describe your encounters?"

"What exactly are you asking?"

"We have taken statements from several people indicating Ms. Yaeger sometimes enjoyed rough sex."

"I see. Well, with me, it was nothing like that. I mean, she was not shy about what she wanted."

"Which was?"

Shannon turned red. "Do I need to spell it out?"

"I'm afraid you do. Of course we could compel you to testify in a deposition. Under oath. Or the police could."

"All right. I get it. Cathy had what I would call a very healthy sexual appetite. Close to insatiable at times."

"But," Jason interjected, "nothing kinky. No leather, nothing like that?"

Shannon looked surprised. No, nothing like that."

"Where did you get together?" Bob asked.

"At my condo is Solana Beach." Solana Beach was a quiet beach town north of the campus.

"Did Cathy ever mention Kenneth Glick?"

"No, never."

"And, this might sound like a strange question, but did she ever mention anything about being in physical pain, needing medication?"

Again Shannon looked surprised. "No, nothing like that. She was quite healthy, as far as I knew."

"Did she sometimes spend the night with you?"

"Yes. A few times."

"And did she have trouble sleeping? Or did you see her take a pill before bed?"

"No, she seemed to sleep well."

"Did she ever mention taking or needing Demerol?"

"Demerol? God, no."

"And we have to ask. Where were you on May the eighteenth and nineteenth?"

Shannon looked at a calendar on his computer.

"In Chicago. At a conference. With about fifty academic colleagues."

"Thank you. I think that's all we need," Bob said. He and Jason got up to leave. "We will need the names of a few of those colleagues at that conference, or perhaps your travel receipts. Just for the record."

"I'll have the secretary show you the travel vouchers."

"Thanks. Strictly routine."

"Will I need to testify in court?" He hesitated. "It would be embarrassing, and maybe damaging, to admit to an affair with a student, even though she was never a student of mine."

"It's hard to say at this point."

"I see."

Bob thanked him for his time.

On the way out, Shannon spoke to the secretary, who showed them copies of the travel vouchers.

28

"I believe him," Jason said, once they had gone back and retrieved his car.

"Yeah, so do I. Except I wonder if he'd admit to kinky sex. With a student."

"Maybe not. But clearly, he didn't kill her."

"No. Not if he was in Chicago."

They both chuckled.

"Of course," Jason said, "if he's a biologist, he might have been able to procure Demerol, and he wouldn't admit it."

Bob hadn't thought of that.

"True. But it doesn't seem likely. He's smart enough to know he could get in a lot of trouble giving a powerful drug to someone."

"Yeah. And he seemed genuinely surprised when we mentioned it."

They were quiet for a few minutes.

"Bob," Jason said, "I'm wondering. Is it possible our client is guilty? I mean, he admits to having a temper. The kinky sex. Last person to see her alive . . ."

"It's possible. My gut says no, but God knows, I could be wrong. But remember, the question for us isn't really if he did it. The question is, can the state prove it? So far, their case seems weak."

Somewhere along the way, Bob had realized, he had stopped caring too much about whether his clients were guilty and more about what the state could and could not prove in court. He didn't trust the DA's office, or the police; he had seen too many cut corners, too many rushes to judgment.

It had bothered him at first, defending people who might be guilty, bothered him a lot. And he still did not take on clients he thought were guilty of something serious from their initial encounter.

But something had definitely shifted in how he thought about his job, the law, the state. He couldn't decide if that made him jaded or smart.

"It makes you both," Marcus had said once when they talked it over. "It means you're doing your job with your eyes open."

Bob hoped that was true.

"Will you call Shannon to testify?" Jason asked.

"Way too early to say. Have you tried to set up a meeting with Cathy's parents?"

"They're resistant, but told me to call them at the end of the week."

Back at the office, Sarah has already bought lunch for

everyone, which they ate at their respective desks. Bob made notes of his conversation with Shannon and made some calls to Anna Mendoza's references, who all sang her praises. He looked over her file one more time, then called and offered her the job.

She was thrilled. Bob told her she could start the following week. She thanked him over and over.

It was time to meet Cathy's neighbor. He and Jason headed out.

29

Rebecca Morrison lived across the way from Cathy's apartment. The building was U-shaped, arranged around a courtyard that contained a concrete table and benches and a few dilapidated lounge chairs. Morrison was a well-dressed woman in her seventies who offered them tea, which they both accepted.

She recounted what she had heard and seen that night. An argument, very loud. Cathy wanted Ken to leave. He pushed into her apartment.

Just as she had told the police.

"I see," Bob said. He asked her if she was sure it was Cathy and Ken she heard and saw.

"Oh yes, it was them."

Morrison brushed her brown hair back from her ear, and Bob saw that she wore a hearing aid. The police transcript hadn't mentioned that.

"Ms. Morrison, tell us, what were you doing just before the argument?"

"I was lying down."

"Did the noise of the argument wake you up?"

"No, I just woke up."

"And then what?"

"I heard voices from the courtyard."

"I see. And were you wearing your hearing aid? Do you take it off when you rest?"

Morrison looked suddenly flustered. "I do sometimes take it off." She seemed lost in thought.

"And are you sure you were wearing it when you heard that argument?"

She looked down.

"Please, Ms. Morrison. A young man has been accused of murder. His whole life is at stake."

She looked away. "Well, I . . . No. I guess I'm not sure if I put it back on."

"So you can't be sure it was Ms. Yaeger and Mr. Glick you heard."

"It was them."

"Ma'am, is it possible it was other people? Different neighbors, perhaps?"

Morrison took a sip of her tea. "Well, I don't know. I suppose it's possible. But I had heard them arguing before."

Bob spoke as gently as he could. "Is it possible, since you might not have been wearing your hearing aid when you were napping, that you assumed it was them, because you had heard them before?"

Morrison thought for a long moment. "Yes, I suppose that's possible. The police never asked about my hearing aid. Am I in trouble now?" She looked alarmed.

"No, no. Not at all. But what we need you to do is to come into the office and repeat what you've told me in front of a stenographer, under oath. Would you be willing to do that?"

"Yes, yes, of course. I'm so sorry to have made a mess."

"It's fine. Would tomorrow work for you? Jason can pick you up."

They made arrangements for Jason to pick her up first thing in the morning.

Bob thanked her. He was smiling broadly as they got in Jason's car and pulled away.

"And that," Jason said, "is why they pay you the big bucks."

30

When he got back to the office, he looked at his watch: 4:30. 7:30 in Danbury. He dialed home. He wanted to know how the chemo went.

His father answered.

"Well, it wasn't fun, but she got through it. She's asleep now. She threw up a couple of times, which is not unusual, the doctor said."

"Only one more, right?"

"That's what they're saying."

"And how are you holding up?"

"Oh you know. One foot in front of the other. How's your case?"

"Making progress. Today I think I may have challenged a key piece of the state's evidence."

"Good for you."

"Tell Mom I called."

"Of course. Do me a favor."

"Anything."

"Check on your brother. He seems—I don't know. At loose ends. I think he was really expecting that job in Washington."

"Will do. Maybe we'll go up, see them, see Jay. He's growing so fast."

"That's what happens. One minute they're in the crib, the next they're handling murder cases."

Bob laughed. "Take care, Dad."

Bob had an uneasy feeling when he got off the phone. He wasn't sure why.

Murder cases always make me a little nuts. Or maybe it's Mom.

He called home; Marcus wasn't back from campus yet. He called and left a message at his campus office, saying he was leaving work and he'd cook dinner.

As he drove, he thought about that word.

Home.

He had just called Danbury, which he thought of as home. And he called the house he shared with Marcus, and thought of that as home as well.

And then he wondered: Would he and Marcus last as long as his parents? Was San Diego home now, and would it always be?

Yes, he decided. It was home now. But not because they owned a house, but because Marcus was there. And Oscar. Maybe they'd be in California forever, maybe they wouldn't.

But if Marcus was there, it was home.

And yes, they would last.

And then a thought hit him, something that had never occurred to him before.

Marcus would die first. He was ten years older.

Of course, you never knew. As his doctor once said, any of us could go tomorrow.

But all things considered, he would probably lose Marcus some day. How would be stand it?

One foot in front of the other.

31

The next morning Rebecca Morrison came in for her deposition. She had dressed up, a crisp suit and high heels, which Bob found endearing.

Under oath, with her words being transcribed, she admitted she couldn't be sure of what she did and did not hear or see on Cathy's doorstep the night she was murdered. She couldn't stop apologizing for forgetting about her hearing aid, and, after her testimony, Bob reassured her that it was a natural mistake. It wasn't, but he appreciated her willingness to come forward, and there was no point in making her feel worse than she already did.

The important thing was that a key piece of prosecution evidence had been severely compromised. The deposition was typed up by the end of the day and a copy was messengered over to Billy Lewis. He called Billy and suggested they meet the next morning. Lewis agreed to meet for breakfast.

They met at the Crest Café in Hillcrest, a place they had been to a few times for lunch when Bob worked for the DA.

"So," Bob said after they ordered.

"With or without a hearing aid," Billy said, "she had heard and seen them before that night. She's not the only witness who will testify to your guy's temper tantrums."

"Billy, for God sake, you know how weak your case is. Where is motive?"

"Temper equals jealousy. Yaeger slept around. Drunken rage. You know that can happen."

"Yes, and Glick knew all about her sex life. Encouraged it. He played around too. It wasn't an exclusive relationship. He readily admits as much. They're young. You remember being young, I assume?"

Lewis said nothing in response.

"And I've spoken to Melinda."

That surprised Lewis.

"She will vouch for Goldstein's accuracy. He has stellar credentials. And she will testify that the combination of drugs and alcohol killed her." They both knew that judges trusted Melinda.

The seemed to shake Lewis a bit. Bob knew what he had said wasn't 100 percent true; Melinda had said it could have killed her, probably did. But that was a split hair at this point, he thought. He knew she needed to talk to Goldstein before reaching a final judgment, read his report, see the photos. See if the corpse yielded any evidence of another cause of death.

"And, Bob went on, "she will testify that the bruises that showed up in the second autopsy could have been the result of something that happened in the few days before that night. You know how credible she is on the witness stand. She has never been wrong. There's reasonable doubt right there."

"We'll see."

Bob assumed Lewis was being pressured to bring the case to trial, no matter what, by the District Attorney, and that the DA was being pressured by Cathy Yeager's well-connected family.

"Okay, have it your way. But we're going to trial, and

you're going to lose."

Lewis smiled. "Whatever you say, counselor."

They paid their bills and walked out together.

"How's Judy?" Bob asked on the sidewalk.

Lewis smiled. "Getting big. But the second time is so much easier. We know what to expect."

"I hope everything will be fine."

"Thanks." And with that, they went in opposite directions to their cars.

32

Bob drove back to his office. The next order of business was an interview with Richard Cartwright, the actor. Sarah had tracked him down through his press agent, and he agreed to a meeting on Saturday at his house in Los Angeles. He'd be filming every day until then.

"I don't know about Cathy Yaeger," Sarah said. "but I'd have slept with him in a minute."

Bob guffawed.

He spent the next few days working on another case. While he did that, Jason continued to talk to the names on the list Kenny had provided, people he or Yaeger had been involved with.

"Lots of sex," he told Bob. "But there was one piece of new information."

Bob's looked up from the notes Jason had prepared of names and dates of the interviews.

"Apparently both Yaeger and Glick were bisexual. Or, I should say, sometimes liked bisexual episodes."

"Really?"

Jason nodded.

Bob was surprised but not entirely shocked. They were experimenting. Or genuinely bisexual. Lots of people their age were, especially these days. He'd have to talk to Kenny about it, certainly, but didn't think it was urgent. It was already clear that both of them had multiple partners.

"Okay, thanks. Have you gotten through the whole list?"

"Just about. No red flags. What about Cartwright? Do you want me to meet you in LA for that?"

"No, it's a Saturday. I can do that one alone. Take the weekend. You can spend some time with your cute Marine."

Jason laughed. "Oh, he's history. Now it's a Navy guy." Jason seemed to have a never-ending supply of young, handsome boyfriends, mostly from the military, which was omnipresent in San Diego. Bob had once asked Jason why he didn't settle down with one of them.

"Oh, you know," he said, "they just want me for my body. For a while."

When Jason said things like that, Bob felt a pang. When he was growing up he always felt like an awkward geek and envied boys, and later men, who looked like Jason, especially once he joined the gay community, where looks counted for so much. But with Jason, he had learned that being gorgeous can be a mixed blessing.

That night, after Greek take-out, Bob told Marcus what Jason had discovered.

"Are you surprised?" Bob asked.

Marcus pondered as he loaded the dishwasher.

"No, not really. When I first met Kenny I thought maybe I picked up a little gay vibe. And these days . . . you know. Gender as a performance. Judith Butler. Eve Sedgwick."

Bob nodded as he put the leftovers in the frig. Butler and Sedgwick were all the rage in academia, and it seemed like a cottage industry of queer theory was taking over much of the humanities, and even some of the social sciences. Bob had tried to read some of Butler's and Sedgwick's work but couldn't cut through their language and style, which seemed to him convoluted to a ridiculous degree. But their ideas had certainly taken hold, permeating the more liberal college campuses. Sexual experimentation of all sorts was becoming more open. More and more kids in their teens and twenties thought of themselves as queer or bisexual.

"Do you think," Bob asked Marcus, "that it's happening more, or that people are just more open about it now?"

"Hard to say. Maybe it's just part of a general nonchalance about sex. Or . . ."

"Or?"

"Or HIV made everyone think and talk more openly about sex. And come up with creative alternatives."

Bob thought that was a really interesting idea, something he hadn't thought about before. It was true, though. AIDS had changed things. Profoundly. And not just for gay men.

"Well, I like the way you perform your gender," Bob said.

"Why Captain Butler, how you talk."

After sex, Bob suggested to Marcus that they drive up to LA together on Friday afternoon and stay with Alex and Carol for a night or two. Marcus liked the idea; he always enjoyed being with Bob's family and being in Los Angeles. He had academic colleagues he could check in with at UCLA, and there was a big city energy in LA that San Diego lacked. Of course, that energy came with horrific traffic, congestion, and, more often than not, bad air. A few nights there was the right amount of time.

33

They arrived at Alex and Carol's house in Santa Monica around 3:30 on Friday afternoon, just as Jay was getting home from school.

"Uncle Bob! Uncle Marcus!" He hugged them both. Sophie, their golden retriever, danced all around them, no doubt smelling Oscar, her puppy, on their clothes. They had just seen Jay a few weeks before, for a Passover seder, but it looked like he had grown another inch. And he looked more and more like his father and like Bob.

Carol and Bob cooked dinner, which they ate out on their patio. It was a balmy night and they could feel the breeze from the ocean, a few blocks away.

After dinner Jay insisted Bob and Marcus come see his new bow and arrow set, which had been set up behind the garage. At day camp the previous summer he had developed a sudden passion for archery. He shot a few arrows and sure enough, hit the bullseye, or came really close.

"Amazing," Bob said.

"It's easy. Want to try?"

"Um, no. But thanks."

"What about you, Uncle Marcus?"

"Well . . ."

Marcus took an arrow, aimed, and hit close to the bullseye.

"Where did you learn to do that?" Bob asked, incredulous.

"One of my many hidden talents."

After Jay went to bed and the weather was cooling down on the patio, the adults had coffee in the living room.

"I talked to Mom today," Alex said. "She sounded fine."

"One more session of chemo, right?" Carol asked.

Alex and Bob simultaneously said "yeah."

That made Carol and Marcus both smile; they sounded so much alike.

"I told her we'd come next weekend, and she all but forbade me."

"Maybe we'll go," Bob said. "Or I will. You can go as soon as Jay finishes school."

"Yes, that makes sense," Carol said.

"Did you talk to Dad?" Bob asked.

"No, he was at the office."

"Well that's a good sign, it means he's less worried."

34

Saturday morning Marcus had breakfast with a colleague from UCLA, so the others had a leisurely breakfast on the patio. Jay had taken Sophie to the local dog park, where, Carol said, she had dozens of friends, both human and canine.

"So, how's work?" Bob asked.

"Oh, you know," Alex said. "Corporate assholes fighting over whose is bigger."

Bob and Carol laughed.

"Seriously," Bob said.

"I am serious. These guys, they graduate from the Harvard or Stanford Business School and they think of themselves as Masters of the Universe. Then they find out they have to compete with five or ten or twenty other guys just like them."

"So, just like Tom Wolfe said." Wolfe's novel, *Bonfire of the Vanities*, had come out a few years earlier and satirized Wall Street and business culture. Though Bob thought Tom

Hanks and Melanie Griffith were miscast, the film version did the same.

"Almost. Only those guys were polite compared to the Hollywood version."

"And so . . . ?"

"And so they maneuver and plot and scheme and end up in court."

"What about the DC option?"

At the mention of DC, Carol's expression changed from a smile to neutral.

"Doesn't seem to be happening. At least not yet."

"Well," Bob said, "you could always take up something calm and restful, like criminal law. Just murder and mayhem, the non-corporate variety."

They all chuckled.

"Dad said this would happen if I joined a big corporate firm out here," Alex said wistfully. "I should have listened."

Bob didn't know what to say; a few awkward moments passed.

"Who are you interviewing today?" Carol asked.

"Richard Cartwright."

Both Alex and Carol looked impressed.

"He can't be a criminal, he's too handsome," Carol said.

Bob laughed. "No, just a witness. I think."

35

Cartwright's house was in West Hollywood, just off Sunset Boulevard. It was a modern, one-story house, set back from the road, with only a few small windows facing the street. Bob parked behind a Porsche in the driveway. He rang the bell.

Cartwright opened the door. He was strikingly handsome, around thirty, with jet-black hair, green eyes, and a patrician nose. He was shorter than Bob expected. He was wearing white linen pants and a green shirt that matched his eyes, and was barefoot. He hadn't shaved, which made him more attractive. When Bob had tried that look once, not shaving every day, he thought it made him look like a derelict.

"Hello, I'm Bob Abramson." He handed Cartwright one of his business cards.

"Yes. Come in." He ushered Bob into a large living room, sparsely furnished with black leather furniture. It overlooked the back yard and a large swimming pool. The place had the feel of a house that had just been bought; Bob could detect the faint smell of fresh paint. Cartwright offered Bob coffee or a drink, both of which he declined.

"Thanks for seeing me. As my assistant indicated, I'm an attorney in San Diego. I've been retained to defend Kenneth Glick, who's been accused of the murder of Catherine Yaeger."

Cartwright nodded and waited.

"A friend of Ms. Yaeger's suggested that you had a relationship with her. Is that the case?"

"A personal relationship, yes."

"I'm afraid I need to ask for details."

"I'm really not comfortable talking about my private life." He crossed his legs.

"I fully understand that, but this is a young man accused of murder. You could be forced to testify." Bob tried to sound gentle.

Cartwright got up and went to a bar tucked into a corner of the room, and poured himself a glass of Calistoga mineral water. He sat back down.

"Yes, I knew Cathy. And Ken."

"Both of them?"

"Yes."

"Was your relationship with Ms. Yaeger intimate?"

"My relationship with both of them was intimate."

Bob tried to hide his surprise. Cartwright certainly had a flair for drama; the line sounded like it could have come from an R-rated movie script. Even the way he had crossed the room seemed like it came from a script.

"How did you meet?"

"I met Cathy at a party in Del Mar, two summers ago."

The small village, north of San Diego, had a popular racetrack, often frequented by Hollywood types.

"Go on, please."

"We got to talking. She said she wanted to be an actress, and we talked about breaking into the business. I suggested she call me if she was ever in LA. I heard from her a few weeks later, and we got together."

"How often did you see her?"

"Maybe seven or eight times."

"Always here?"

"Sometimes at my place in Palm Springs."

"Have you ever been to her apartment in San Diego?"

"No. In fact, I've never been to San Diego."

"And what about Mr. Glick?"

"Once he drove Cathy to Palm Springs, and I noticed him sitting in his car in front of the house. So I invited him in."

"And?"

"And we all had a drink, and one thing led to another."

"Just so I'm absolutely clear, you had sex with both of them. Together."

"I'd put it this way. Kenny and I both had sex with Cathy at the same time." Again, Cartwright kept his voice neutral. A cool customer, Bob thought.

"How often did you see them together?"

Cartwright thought for a moment. "Maybe three times."

"And how would you describe their relationship with each other?"

"They seemed fine. Comfortable together."

Bob chose his words very carefully. "Did you ever see Mr. Glick act aggressively toward Ms. Yaeger?"

"Sexually, yes. But so was I. Nothing that was . . . "

"Nothing that was . . . ?"

"Alarming. At least not to me. I wouldn't have allowed it if there was. Cathy was . . ." His voice trailed off again.

"Yes?"

"Enthusiastic. Whatever we did."

Cartwright got up, refilled his glass with Calistoga. He stood by the bar and faced Bob with the hint of a smirk on his gorgeous face.

What part is he playing now? Bob wondered.

"Look," Cartwright went on. "They were both very attractive. Young. A bit on the wild side. We enjoyed each other. That's really all I'm prepared to say. They . . ."

"Yes?"

"They performed well. They knew what they were doing. They were not innocents. I think we all had a good time, and that's really all it was."

"Okay. Just for the record, where were you on May eighteenth and nineteenth?"

Cartwright got up and went to another room, and returned with what looked like a Filofax calendar.

"That was a Wednesday and Thursday. I was filming at

Universal. All day both days. Driver picked me up at seven a.m., and I was there until, I don't know, maybe seven p.m. Days on film sets are long. When I got home my assistant was here, cooking dinner."

"Just for the sake of completeness, I'll need names of people who can verify that."

"That's fine. If your secretary calls this number on Monday, my assistant can give her that information." He handed Bob a card out of a pocket in the Filofax. "Tell her to call the second number listed."

Bob thanked him.

"One thing. I'd really appreciate it if I could be kept out of any trial or publicity. You know, Hollywood. Your image is your paycheck. Studios aren't so big on anything . . . like this." He laughed a bit and smiled a dazzling smile. He was trying to act nonchalant, but it wasn't working. By this point, a director would have asked for more takes.

"We'll try to keep this quiet. But this is a serious murder investigation."

"I know. Horrible thing, someone like Cathy dying that way."

"If we need to talk again," Cartwright said as Bob stood up, "please contact my attorney." He handed him another card.

"I will. Thank you for your time."

Cartwright saw him to the door.

36

Bob drove back to Santa Monica. Clearly, he had a lot to talk to Kenny about. And he was not happy that Kenny had been holding things back. Cartwright's name had come from Beth, Cathy's friend at Diversionary. His name should have been on Kenny's list, and wasn't.

Bob kept thinking about what Cartwright had said. Perhaps it was just that he was an actor, so using certain language came naturally. Or did it imply more? Bob kept turning the phrase over and over in his mind.

They performed well.

Cathy was an ambitious actor. A Hollywood contact could be crucial. They met at a party, and things proceeded from there. But was Cathy exchanging sexual favors for help with her career, either real or imagined? Did Cartwright promise to introduce her around town? Or did he string her along, knowing that would be on her mind?

Or was it just that Cartwright was gorgeous?

When he got back to Santa Monica, Carol, Jay, and Marcus were playing Monopoly out on the patio. Sophie was napping under the table, just like Oscar did. Alex was working in his home office.

"Who's winning?"

"I am," Jay beamed.

"And I'm in jail," Marcus said. "I think they loaded the dice."

Carol laughed. "I'm calling game over."

That night they left Jay with a sitter, a high school girl who lived down the block, and the four adults went to a new French bistro Carol said they had been wanting to try. The place was packed and the food was terrific.

"We only got a reservation because they had a cancellation right before I called. Usually there's at least a month's wait. And I begged," she said with a laugh.

After the main course, a well-dressed woman walked in

with an entourage, noticed Alex, and came over and said hello. Alex stood up and introduced everyone to Shirley Cox, a member of the State legislature.

"She's definitely someone on the way up," Alex said after she went back to her table.

"Are you thinking about running for something?" Bob asked.

"I was. Or am. Not sure."

"Would Clinton endorse you? You did a lot for him here. You raised so much money."

"I was hoping he might. But he stays out of local or lower-level state races."

Bob realized their father was right, Alex was sounding unsure about his direction. He was thirty-five, five years older than Bob; a midlife crisis could be in the offing. Bob was confident it wouldn't involve running off with another woman or anything like that. But career-wise, it was hard to say. He felt for his brother and wished he knew how to help him.

"I did just join a state Human Rights Council. That may give me some useful contacts."

Carol put her hand on top of Alex's. They ordered dessert.

37

On Sunday morning Marcus made his famous French toast, which Jay loved, and they said their goodbyes.

"Uncle Marcus, can I come visit? I want to go to the zoo again."

"Of course you can. We'll figure out when." Jay hugged

both Bob and Marcus as they put their travel bags in the car.

They got home around 2:00 and found a message from Sarah on the machine: *I tracked down Alex Johnson. He refused to meet.*

It was followed by another message, from Jason: *After Sarah talked to Johnson, I contacted him and did my tough cop act. I reminded him he could be subpoenaed. He said he'd have to talk to his attorney. Then he called me back and said he would agree to an off-the-record interview with his lawyer present. He's going away for a week and is willing to meet week after next.*

They picked up Oscar from the kennel, who went crazy at seeing them and was so excited when he got home they had to play endless games of fetch in the yard to wear him out. He finally settled down and took a nap until he smelled Bob cooking dinner, when he assumed his usual position next to whoever was cooking. Marcus went out to do their weekly shopping while Bob whipped up some of his excellent lasagna.

"Jay really is getting big," Marcus said over dinner.

"Yeah. And he seems so happy." Bob paused. "Would you ever . . ."

"Hmm?"

"Would you ever think about adopting a child?"

Marcus put down his fork. They had never discussed the idea. It had never even occurred to him.

"I don't know," he said honestly.

"We could do what Miles and Steve did, adopt from overseas."

"Is it something you want?" Marcus asked.

"Maybe. I don't know."

"I don't know either. We'd have to think about it. It wouldn't be something we should do on a whim."

"No. Clearly."

They were both quiet for a long minute.

"Maybe," Marcus said, "we should talk it over with Miles and Steve. Get their perspective."

"That's a good idea. Let's invite them over for dinner. We owe them an invitation anyway."

Marcus got up and kissed the top of Bob's head, then started clearing away the dishes. He realized it meant something that Bob thought they were solid enough as a couple to think about doing this. And they were.

And then he had a thought. He wondered if Bob was thinking about a child because of his mother's cancer.

38

On Monday morning at the office Bob called Kenny, and a woman answered the phone. When Kenny came on the line, Bob said he needed to see him. They arranged to meet at 4:00.

When they got in, he told Sarah and Jason to stop working on weekends unless it was really necessary.

"I don't pay you enough to work 24/7."

They both laughed.

He spent the rest of the day working on a brief for another case with Anna. His new clerk had a lot of good suggestions, and Bob was happy he had hired her. He took her to lunch and asked her about her family. It turned out that her grandparents on both sides came to the United States illegally, but, despite having next to nothing, were determined that their children succeed. Her father was a doctor and her mother a social worker here in town. Bob marveled at their story. Anna asked for the afternoon off; she needed to sign the lease on her new apartment. Bob agreed readily and went back to the office.

Kenny arrived promptly at 4:00. Bob told Jason to sit in on the interview; he wanted Kenny to feel on the spot.

"Ken, I was in LA over the weekend, and I spoke to Richard Cartwright."

Kenny looked embarrassed. "Oh."

"Yes. 'Oh.' First question: Why was he not on your list of sexual contacts?"

Kenny squirmed. "Well, he's famous. He has a lot to lose."

"So do you, Ken. You've been charged with murder. Murder. That's not a traffic ticket."

Kenny looked away. Bob went on.

"I need to know everything about your relationship with Cathy. Everything. I can't defend you otherwise."

"Okay. I'm sorry."

"Cartwright said you drove Cathy to Palm Springs to see him."

"That's right."

"Did you ever drive Cathy to other meetings?"

"Yes. A few."

"I will need those names."

"I only knew Richard's name because he's famous. I don't really know who the other guys were."

Jason spoke. "Could you drive back to their places? We could find out who they were that way."

"Yes, I suppose."

Bob resumed the questioning. He got up and circled around Kenny's chair; he wanted him to feel intimidated.

"Were these other meetings also three-ways, as with Cartwright?"

"A few, yes. Sometimes I just sat in the car, or went and had a cup of coffee."

"And how were these meetings set up?"

"Word of mouth, mostly."

"Explain."

"One guy mentions Cathy's name to a friend, he calls her."

"You said mostly. How else?"

"Sometimes we ran an ad in one of the trashy LA weeklies. Or Cathy did."

"I see." Bob wanted to start shouting but didn't. He sat back down and looked Kenny in the eye with his best scary lawyer stare.

"Did you or Cathy ever ask for money for these . . . sessions?"

"No! I swear. It was just sex. And for Cathy, networking. A lot of these guys had Hollywood connections."

"Is that the truth, Kenny? Because if it isn't, the police may find out, so you might as well tell me now."

"It's the truth."

"Isn't Cathy's father a studio exec? Isn't that enough of a Hollywood connection?"

"He didn't want her going into the business. He was really firm about that. She felt . . ."

"She felt?"

"Abandoned."

"I see."

Bob looked at Jason, which Jason understood to mean they needed to talk to Cathy's parents. Jason had been trying to set up a meeting with them.

"Look," Kenny said. "These were just adventures. Sexual adventures. Cathy called it research." He smiled an unconvincing smile.

"Did you and Cathy meet with Alex Johnson?"
"Yes."
"How many times?"
"A few. I didn't keep count."
"How did you make that connection?"
"Through James Cunningham."

Bob sat back in his chair, in shock. But then, after a moment, he was not entirely surprised. He knew Cunningham from the previous case. Cunningham was Johnson's stepson. He knew from the previous case that Cunningham had sexual tastes that ran toward the intense.

"Did you have relations with Cunningham?"
"Yes."
"Separately or together?"
"Sometimes the three of us. And sometimes separately."
"How did you meet Cunningham?"
"Actually we met him at the theater one night, the Old Globe, during intermission. It was just a chance meeting." The Old Globe was one of San Diego's premier theaters.

"Is there anything else you're not telling me? Now is the time."

"No, I don't think so. I'm really sorry about this."

"I want you to go with Jason now and arrange to go on a tour of houses where some of these trysts took place. I assume you met Cunningham at his beach house in Carlsbad?" Bob had been there.

Kenny nodded.

"One more thing. Who answered the phone when I called you this morning?"

Kenny turned bright read. "Just someone I met casually."

"No sex, casual or otherwise, until the trial is over. No dating. I mean it. The police could be watching your every move."

"Okay."

"That's it for today. No more secrets. Understood?"

Kenny nodded. He looked relieved to get up and leave.

39

The next day, a Tuesday, Bob had Jason contact Cathy's parents again, and they finally agreed to meet that afternoon at their beach house in Laguna Beach, about an hour north of San Diego. Bob and Jason drove up in Jason's car.

The house was perched on a cliff overlooking a beautiful stretch of sand south of Laguna's hub. A man they assumed to be Cathy's father opened the front door when they knocked.

"Hello. I'm Robert Yaeger. Come in."

He ushered them into a simply but tastefully furnished living room with a stunning view. The windows were open and the smell of the ocean filled the room. Looking at the house, knowing this was a second home, there was no doubt that Cathy came from impressive wealth.

"This is my wife, Deborah. Please, have a seat." Deborah smiled a thin smile.

Robert was the picture of a successful corporate executive, tall, silver-haired, tan. Deborah was a beautiful woman in her fifties. Their clothes were simple, tasteful. Deborah looked familiar but Bob couldn't think of what her stage name had been or what film or television show she had been in.

"Thank you for seeing us. And let me say how sorry we are for your loss."

"Thank you," Deborah said. The Yaegers were drinking coffee and offered them a cup, which both men declined.

"As you know, I've been retained to defend Kenneth Glick. The state has charged him with the murder, but, based on what I've seen of their evidence, their case is very weak."

"So you don't think he's guilty?" Robert asked.

"No, I don't."

"We're not sure ourselves," Deborah said.

Bob and Jason glanced at each other.

"Can you explain why," Bob asked.

Deborah spoke. "Cathy was happy with Ken. She said they got along really well. He was her first boyfriend that lasted more than a month or so. They were beginning to think about moving in together."

"Had you met Mr. Glick?"

"I met him first," Robert said. "I was down in San Diego on business and the three of us had lunch. About three or four months ago. He seemed okay. No red flags."

"After that," Deborah said, "we had them here in Laguna for dinner, a month or so later. I liked him. I was happy for Cathy." Her eyes started to water.

"Thank you for sharing that. We've heard from someone who knew Cathy that you were opposed to Cathy continuing to act. Is that true?"

Robert refilled his coffee cup from a carafe. "Yes, it's true. I discouraged her. It's a brutal business. I've seen what it can do to people. The film industry is full of talented people, good performers, who don't make it, through no fault of their own. It's just so damn competitive. For every screen roll there are at least twenty-five actors who could play the part and do it well. Maybe fifty."

"Did you feel the same way, Mrs. Yaeger?"

"Well, yes, although I thought she could teach drama, or something up that alley. She loved children. When she was younger she babysat for neighbors all the time and talked about wanting a large family. Or I thought she could work on the stage. But Hollywood, no. I didn't want that for her. I tried it for a while and gave up. It was just too hard."

"I see. Was Cathy in good health, as far as you know?"

Her parents looked at each other. They were clearly surprised by the question.

"Yes," Deborah said slowly. "She was perfectly healthy."

"I ask because the San Diego medical examiner found the drug Demerol in her system. If you're not familiar with it, it's a powerful pain medication, sometimes also prescribed for sleep."

"They didn't tell us that," Robert said. "They just told us the San Diego authorities found an 'accidental death.' They didn't say much more. It just didn't make sense. Our lawyer couldn't get the autopsy report itself. Someone still needed to sign off on it, apparently."

"Yes, that would be Melinda Ivanov, the city's chief Medical Examiner. She was called out of the country due to illness in the family."

"Ah. That explains it. That's why we asked for another autopsy when they surrendered the body, we were suspicious. And it found . . . what it found."

"I see." Again Bob and Jason glanced at each other.

"Someone must have drugged her," Deborah said.

"We don't think there's evidence against Mr. Glick, other than the fact that they were seeing each other. At this point, it's unclear how the drug got into her system, or when the violence against her occurred. It could have been a day or two earlier, which is why it didn't appear in the first autopsy. Those kinds of bruises can take some time to develop."

"No one told us that either," Robert said, getting upset.

Deborah looked pensive.

"I've spoken to Dr. Ivanov. She believes the combination of drugs and alcohol really was the cause of death. She is very good at her job. She's never been mistaken in the past."

"It's possible, isn't it," Robert said, "that someone drugged her and then . . . did those things to her. Maybe that morning? There's no security where she lives."

"Yes, it's possible."

"Did Cathy ever give any indication that Mr. Glick could be violent in any way?"

"Never," Deborah said, sounding surprised. "I think she would have told me. We were close. Or she would have dropped him."

"Are the police pursuing this any further?" Robert asked.

"Not as far as I know. They are convinced they arrested the right person. But we're pursuing various leads, and hope to find out what really happened."

Robert nodded. Deborah looked away.

"In the weeks leading up to her death, were you in touch with Cathy?"

"We talked at least once a week," Deborah said.

"And did she sound like herself? Was anything bothering her?"

"She seemed fine. Normal. Happy." At that, Deborah started to cry. She dabbed her eyes with a tissue and her husband took her hand.

"If there's nothing else . . ." Robert said.

"No, that's what we needed to ask. Thank you for seeing us. And again, we are incredibly sorry for your loss."

Robert walked them to the door. Bob gave him a business card and asked him to call if they thought of anything else that might be relevant.

"Sorry to chase you out, but this is very difficult for my wife."

"Of course. We understand."

40

"That was interesting," Jason said after they were on the road.

"Yes, very," Bob replied.

"They liked Glick. And she had no health problems. And they didn't know anything about their daughter's secret life."

"Right. If this goes to trial, they would be in for a shock. A bad one."

"So where does that leave us?"

"Looking for a suspect. Doing the work the police should be doing."

"Yeah," Jason said, sounding something between disgusted and resigned.

They were mostly quiet on the drive south. Jason dropped Bob at the office, where he checked in with Sarah. He took home papers he needed for the next morning, a trial in court on another case, a bogus charge of child abuse after a nasty divorce.

The trial lasted most of the day, and the judge ended up dismissing the charge for lack of evidence, as Bob had hoped. The judge even scolded the prosecutor, someone Bob did not know, for bringing the case to court. Bob tried not to gloat as he left the courtroom.

He went home early, anxious to hear about his mother's second dose of chemo. He assumed there would be a phone call. Marcus came home and cooked his tuna casserole, and they waited, distractedly watching TV.

Around 8:00, the phone finally rang. It was Bob's father.

"Bobby, it's not good."

"What? What?"

"Before the infusion they did some tests, blood tests. There were some results the doctor thought were strange. So after the chemo, they did some scans. The doctor had them do them right away."

Bob waited, his eyes closed.

"There's some cancer in her lung. It's unusual for it to spread like this so quickly, but it happens."

Bob swallowed hard. "So what happens now?"

"Surgery. In New Haven, at Yale hospital."

"When?"

"Friday."

"What are they saying about. . . ." He couldn't finish the sentence.

"They're not saying. Listen. I need you to call Alex and Carol."

"Of course. We'll fly out. We'll figure out a schedule."

"Okay."

"Dad, it could be all right. At least they found it."

"Yes. It could be all right." He didn't sound like he believed it. "I have to get off the phone. Your mother didn't even want me to call until after the surgery."

They hung up.

Bob walked out to the living room.

"What is it?" Marcus could tell something was wrong. Bob told him.

"Oh, Jesus."

"I need to call Alex."

Marcus got up and poured Bob a scotch. They both mostly stayed away from hard liquor except when trouble was brewing. Then they broke out the hard stuff.

"Here. Drink this first."

Bob did, in one gulp. He went into the kitchen and dialed Alex's number.

Carol answered.

"Carol, hi. Is Alex home? Ask him to pick up on another extension."

Alex said nothing when Bob gave him the news. Finally Carol spoke. "Okay. I'll fly out tomorrow. You guys fly out when you can, on Friday or the weekend."

Bob and Alex said "okay" simultaneously.

"Jay can stay with Marcus over the weekend. He'll love that. Maybe on Monday Marcus can come up and stay here, get Jay to school. Or I'll fly back. We'll figure it out."

Again, a simultaneous "okay."

"Let's stick with the facts," Carol went on. "It could be fine. The important thing right now is helping them get through the next few days." Both Bob and Marcus had always admired Carol's level-headedness. She was the person you wanted around in a crisis.

Like Ruth.

"Yes," Bob said. He thought at one point he heard a sob from Alex.

They hung up. Bob told Marcus the plan. "Is that okay?"

"Of course. I can cancel my classes next week, stay in LA if I need to."

Bob started to cry. Marcus took his hand, led him to the bathroom, and drew a bath. Bob took off his clothes, dropping them on the floor, and got into the tub. Marcus sat on the edge.

Oscar, who never came into the bathroom, could tell something was wrong. He pushed open the bathroom door with his nose and lay down, half in, half out, facing the tub.

41

Neither of them slept very well. Bob tossed and turned. Around 3:00 a.m. they both got up and drank mint tea.

"I can fly out today. Everything in the office can wait."

"Okay."

Bob seemed a bit more relaxed so they went back to bed.

At 5:30, Marcus woke up again. Bob was on the phone in the kitchen, making an airline reservation. They took turns in the shower and then ate frozen waffles for breakfast. Bob packed a bag. His flight was at 11:00.

"I'll stop at the office, then leave my car at the airport. Call Alex, figure out what to do about Jay. You could go up. Or he could come down. Maybe he could take the train, he'd like that." There was a train from Union Station in LA to downtown San Diego. "The dogs, you'll have to figure out what to do with the dogs."

Marcus nodded. "Don't worry. We'll be fine here. Call me when you know what's what."

Bob nodded. He gathered his things, kissed Marcus, and left. On the way to the office, he started to cry. Really cry.

"Pull yourself together," he said out loud to himself. "They need you."

He slept on the plane, which landed at JFK at 8:00 local time. He rented a car and got to Danbury close to 10:30. Carol opened the front door. They hugged.

Ruth and Jake were in the den.

"Hi, honey," Ruth said, as Bob bent down to kiss her. Jake got up and hugged him. There were the remnants of peach pie on the coffee table, one of Ruth's specialties.

"Did you eat?" Ruth asked.

"Lunch, on the plane."

"You must be starved, come into the kitchen." She started to get up.

"Don't get up, I'll bring a plate," Carol said.

"Not too much, I'm not really hungry." She returned with a plate of pasta salad.

He ate a few bites.

"Alex will fly in Friday, he has to be in court tomorrow," Carol announced. Everyone nodded.

"What about Jay?" Ruth asked.

"Alex's paralegal will pick him up from school and drive him down to San Diego, with Sophie."

"Sophie and Oscar together, I'd pay to see that," Jake said, and everyone chuckled.

"Okay, so what are the doctors saying?" Bob asked after a few more bites.

"Well," Ruth said, "they think it's a small lesion in the left lung, and that they can remove it. They're hopeful."

Bob tried to smile.

"How long will you be in the hospital?"

"They're not saying, it'll depend on exactly what they see."

"And after the surgery?"

"Possibly radiation. They're not sure."

The word hung in the air like a bad smell.

"Look," Ruth said. "this happens to women. One in nine. I mean the breast cancer. They know what they're doing."

"How was the chemo?"

"Not as bad as the first time."

Jake shot him a look that said, don't believe it.

"I'm heading to bed," Ruth said. "You guys are on California time, you're not tired yet. The chemo does make you tired."

Everyone stood up. Bob kissed her again. Jake said he'd be up soon.

Everyone sat down again.

"So . . . how bad is it, really?" Bob asked.

"They don't know. The doctor was shocked it was in the lung, it was at such an early stage in the breast. But the good news is that now they will be vigilant, they know to watch her carefully, and act fast."

Bob and Carol nodded.

"I wanted to take her to Sloan Kettering for a second opinion, but she wouldn't hear of it, she likes these doctors. The oncologist here got us a surgeon at Yale Med."

"If it gets complicated," Bob said, his voice cracking, "take her to Sloan. Insist."

Jake nodded. "I'm going up."

Carol started carrying dishes into the kitchen, and Bob got up to help. "There's more pie if you want." Bob shook his head. "Alex is a basket case. After you called the other night, he walked into a door. Twice."

"I'm pretty shook up myself."

"I'm sure. But you need to take it one step at a time. One day at a time. It's the only way to get through something like this."

Bob nodded. Carol had been through something like this with her father, who lived in Minneapolis. He was fine, at least at the moment.

They loaded the dishwasher and Carol said she was going

up. She leaned down and kissed him on the cheek.

Bob sat up for a while. He called Marcus, and they talked about what to do with Jay over the weekend. They'd do the zoo on Saturday, Marcus said, and they'd figure something out for Sunday. Maybe dog beach.

"Sophie and Oscar reunited. Take pictures."

Marcus laughed. "I love you. Enough to take care of two dogs."

42

On Thursday Ruth had pre-surgery tests; Jake went with her while Carol and Bob went grocery shopping and cooked as much food as they could, things that would keep in the fridge for a few days or that could be frozen. Bob made two large trays of lasagna.

When Jake brought Ruth home around 3:00, she looked around the kitchen and asked if they had decided to open a restaurant.

Ruth took a nap while Jake went to his study to check in at his office. They had an early dinner and everyone went to bed early, since Ruth needed to report to the hospital at 6:30 the next morning.

No one slept well. Everyone was putting on a brave face. At 4:30 a.m. they all got up. Ruth couldn't eat anything before the surgery; the others quickly had toast and coffee and then they left for the hospital. Everyone hugged Ruth. Bob and Carol went to the waiting room; Jake went with Ruth as far as the doctors would allow, and then joined them.

They sat and waited. From time to time Carol and

brought coffee with bagels or cookies from the cafeteria. Jake and Bob drank the coffee but didn't touch the food. They talked very little.

At 12:30, the surgeon came out in his scrubs. As he approached, they all stood. Jake took Bob's hand, something he hadn't done since Bob was in fifth grade.

"Good news. It was a very small lesion. We were able to excise all of it and we got very good margins, which is important in cases like this. I recommend some radiation treatments to make absolutely sure there is no recurrence at that spot."

Jake closed his eyes and nodded. "How long will you keep her here?"

"Around three days, perhaps less. It will depend on how quickly the incision heals."

Jake nodded again.

"While this is good news, and I don't want to worry you excessively, we will need to keep a close eye on her to make sure there are no mets anywhere else."

"Mets?" Bob asked.

"Metastases."

Everyone nodded.

"Your oncologist will discuss all of that with you. It will mean periodic tests and scans, nothing intrusive. The important thing to keep in mind is that in the vast majority of these cases, the cancer can be stopped if we catch it on time. And she may be completely fine from this point on."

"Thank you so much, Doctor." Jake shook his hand with both of his.

"She should be awake in an hour or so. I suggest you get some food and then come back here; a nurse will find you when she's awake. She'll be groggy, and fairly heavily sedated, so be prepared."

The doctor left them in the lobby. Jake let out a deep breath.

"I'll go call Alex," Carol said.

"And I'll call Marcus."

Another family, also waiting tensely, said there was a courtesy phone in the adjacent room.

Carol spoke with Alex's secretary, who said Alex was planning to take the red-eye that night. Bob reached Marcus at home.

"Oh thank God, Pinky. That's about as good as the news could be."

"Yes, I suppose."

"It is. It really is."

43

Alex himself delivered Jay and Sophie to San Diego around 6:30; he had decided to fly out of San Diego and leave his car at the airport there.

Jay was, as predicted, super-excited. "Uncle Marcus!" he shouted, hugging him hard.

Sophie and Oscar were in ecstasy, dancing around each other, sniffing each other, howling. Marcus let them out in the yard where they frolicked, then fed them both.

He had ordered Italian food for all of them, thinking all kids love spaghetti. Jay talked about school and about how excited he was to go back to the zoo.

At 9:00 Alex left for the airport. He hugged and kissed Jay and told him to be good, and he hugged Marcus and thanked him over and over.

"Don't be silly," Marcus said, looking at Jay. "We're going to have a great time."

Jay beamed.

After playing a round of gin rummy, Marcus put Jay to bed on the couch in Bob's study.

"Is Grandma Ruth going to be okay?"

"Yes. Absolutely. She had surgery today but it went really well. She'll need to recover from the surgery, which will take a while, but today was a really good day."

"That's good. Daddy's been crying."

"Well, he was worried. Grandma Ruth is his mom. Everyone cares about their mom."

Jay nodded, looking serious.

Sophie jumped onto the couch with Jay, and Marcus decided to let her stay there.

"She does this all the time at home," Jay explained. "Mom tries to keep her off the bed but she just waits until Mom leaves and jumps back up. Don't tell Mom."

Marcus laughed, wished them good night, and turned out the lights. Sophie rested her head on Jay's stomach and he put his hand on top of her head.

Marcus looked at them and felt something he had never really felt before. He smiled to himself.

He remembered that moment for a long time.

44

While Marcus took Jay to the San Diego Zoo on Saturday and to Dog Beach on Sunday morning, both of which Jay loved, Ruth began her recovery from surgery

3,000 miles away. She was groggy for the first day or so but in good spirits, and by Sunday was joking with the nurses and telling Bob, Carol, and Alex to go home.

"I'll be fine. I'll lose weight from your father's cooking, but I'll be fine."

Alex flew home on Sunday, picking up Jay and Sophie in San Diego. Marcus could tell Ruth's situation had taken a toll on Alex, but he didn't want to ask any questions in front of the boy. When they left, Jay hugged Marcus hard and kissed him on the cheek.

Carol and Bob stayed in Danbury a few more days. The doctors let Ruth go home on Tuesday morning. At home she mostly slept. Bob flew home on Wednesday, Carol on Thursday.

On the plane home, Bob's emotions broke through; until then, he had been on automatic pilot, as he often was in court, just doing what needed to be done—cooking, cleaning the house, grocery shopping, playing cards with Ruth when she was awake. But on the plane, as soon as the seat-belt sign turned off, he got up, went into the tiny bathroom, and cried. He wasn't sure why; the news about Ruth was about as good as it could be, under the circumstances. But he let himself cry.

When he went back to his seat, the kind-looking woman next to him asked him if he was all right.

"I'm okay," he said, trying to smile, wiping his eyes. "My mother in Connecticut just had surgery. They say she should be fine, I don't know why I'm crying."

"Because you love her, and don't want to lose her," his seat-mate said.

Bob smiled. "Yes, you're right."

"So San Diego is home?"

"Yes. Now."

That word again.

They chatted on through the meal service, and after the airplane food Bob was able to nap. He woke only when he heard the captain announce their descent into San Diego.

Marcus picked him up from the airport, leaving the dog at home. Oscar was happy to see him when they got home, though he seemed a bit subdued. Bob looked at Marcus.

"I think he misses Jay and Sophie. He really loved having them here. You should have seen them at Dog Beach."

Bob smiled and got down on the floor, cuddling Oscar, who licked his face.

"Oscar, we're not getting another dog, sorry, buddy."

They ordered pizza and Bob conked out early, still on East Coast time.

He was up early the next morning and left for the office, where he was sure a pile of messages was waiting for him.

And he was right. He plowed through the easy things first. Sarah, Jason, and Anna arrived and they met together. Anna had done a good job of keeping things on track, as much as she could. The big news was that Jason had arranged an interview with Alex Johnson for Friday. Johnson didn't want to meet in LA, so he said he would drive down and take a suite at the Hotel del Coronado, the grand old San Diego hotel on the ocean, and that he'd come alone.

"I assume he doesn't want to be seen anywhere in LA, talking to a lawyer," Jason said.

"Odd. It's not like anyone would know I'm a lawyer."

"Well you've got that look," Sarah said.

"What look?"

"You know. That Ivy-League-transplanted-to-California-what-am-I-doing-here look."

Bob laughed. "And that says 'lawyer'?"

"Lawyer or doctor. Yes."

Anna and Jason both nodded.

"I guess I have to change my wardrobe."

"Maybe flowered shirts," Jason suggested.

"Oh yeah. Judges will love that."

He spent the rest of the day and the next catching up on various cases. When he called Ruth on Thursday evening, she sounded okay.

"I'm baking again. I'll send you poppy seed cake."

45

The next day, Bob took Anna to lunch; he had asked her to dig into Johnson's life and history, see if anything interesting or relevant came up.

"Well, it's an interesting family," she said after they ordered. "Both sides were originally Jewish."

That piqued Bob's interest. "Really?"

"Yes. Itzkowitz on his mother's side, Jacobs on his father's side. All of his grandparents were born in Ukraine or Poland. His parents were born here, first generation. He grew up in Sherman Oaks, in the Valley."

"And who changed the name?"

"Johnson did, when he got to college. He was originally Arnold Jacobs, became Alexander Johnson when he arrived at Pomona on scholarship."

"Clearly a determined young man. What did his father do?"

"He ran a modest dress shop."

"I see. And does Johnson deny being Jewish?"

"He apparently now says he was brought up Methodist."

"Oh." Bob said. "And now he's married to a Cunningham."

Bob was lost in thought. He himself didn't feel particularly Jewish, and his family was not really observant. But they never denied their background, or pretended to be anything they weren't. Both he and his brother had bar mitzvahs.

"I guess that's one way," Bob finally said, "to find the American dream."

"My mother once said something interesting about that when I was young," Anna said.

Bob raised his eyebrows.

"'The American dream. There's the long way, and then there are the shortcuts.' So I asked her what the shortcuts were."

Bob smiled. "And what did she say?"

"She smiled and said the shortcuts don't work for people like us."

The Friday meeting with Johnson took place at 2:00 at the hotel in Coronado. Bob and Jason drove together over the Coronado Bridge, which provided picture-postcard views of the San Diego skyline and the bay. The ocean sparkled.

Bob said something about how he loved the view.

"Yeah, it's great," Jason said. "Of course, there's an earthquake fault right under the bridge."

"It's amazing, Jason. You look like Tab Hunter but sound like Vincent Price."

"Always happy to help."

Johnson had taken a suite in the old, wooden section of the hotel, elegantly furnished with views of the ocean and sand. He was a well-dressed man of about 60, trim, with brown hair that, Bob assumed, must be dyed. He had ordered a tray of coffee and cookies.

"Help yourself, gentlemen."

They arranged themselves in three overstuffed chairs.

"I understand you want to talk to me about the death of Catherine Yaeger."

"Yes," Bob said. "As you know, Kenneth Glick has been charged with her murder. I'm representing him."

Johnson nodded.

"What was the nature of your relationship with Ms. Yaeger and Mr. Glick?"

"It was sexual."

"How did you meet?"

"We met at a small soirée at the home of my wife's son."

"James Cunningham."

"Yes."

"And?"

"And they seemed like an amiable couple, both very attractive, and I suggested they contact me next time they were in Los Angeles. I gave them my card."

"And when was this?"

"Roughly a year ago."

"What happened next?"

"About a month later, Mr. Glick telephoned and suggested a meeting."

"Where did you meet?"

"I took a suite at the Beverly Wilshire."

"And, just to be clear, the three of you were together, sexually."

"Yes, on that occasion, and once more. And I saw Catherine alone a few times."

"And?"

"And what? I have a healthy sexual appetite. I am younger than my wife. She knows I have . . . extra-curricular activities."

"I see."

"In fact, she approves."

"Would you call any of your sessions rough or violent?"

"Certainly not."

"Did you get any sense of trouble or tension between the two of them?"

"No, not at all."

"For the record, where were you on May 18th and 19th?"

Johnson retrieved a small pocket calendar from the pocket of his linen suit.

"We were in Santa Fe. I'm on the board of the Opera there. If you call the Opera manager's office, they can confirm."

"I see. Is there anything else you can add that might shed light on what happened to Ms. Yaeger?"

"I'm afraid I can't. We had a perfectly pleasant, mutually beneficial relationship."

"How," Jason spoke for the first time, "would you say it was beneficial to Mr. Glick or Ms. Yaeger?" He glanced at Bob.

"Well, I was rather generous."

"You paid them?" Bob asked.

"It wasn't payment arranged in advance, or anything of that sort. I offered them tips."

"Tips?"

"Yes."

"How generous were the tips, if you don't mind my asking?"

"It was $500 when I got together with both of them, after that, $300 to Catherine."

"And this was paid in cash?"

"Yes. Of course."

"I see."

"Obviously, gentlemen, I would prefer that none of this be made public. It would be embarrassing for me and for my wife."

"We will do our best to keep this quiet, but I can't promise that. Have the police contacted you?"

"No. I hadn't heard from anyone before you contacted me."

"I see. Well, thank you for your candor."

"You're quite welcome. Glad to help."

And with that, Johnson stood and saw them to the door.

46

On the drive back to the office, Bob asked Jason if there had been any hint of payment from anyone else he had interviewed.

"No. No one mentioned money. Of course, most people wouldn't volunteer that kind of information. And I take it Glick didn't mention 'tips'?"

"No. And he's really beginning to piss me off."

"Interesting that Johnson was careful to say the payments weren't solicited."

"Yeah. He must know that solicitation would mean Ken and Cathy committed a crime. As it is, at least as he describes it, it's somewhat murky, legally speaking."

"He was awfully matter of fact," Jason said. "In an almost creepy way."

Bob thought for a moment. "The rich are different. He knows he could hire an army of well-dressed lawyers to argue he did nothing illegal."

"Would that hold up?"

"It would depend on what Glick said, but yeah, probably."

"And he was awfully quick with 'certainly not' when we asked him about rough stuff. Maybe too quick."

"Yeah. I had the same thought."

They were both quiet for a minute.

"Of course, there could be a possible motive for murder here," Jason said.

"You mean, maybe Glick or Yaeger started blackmailing him. I thought that too."

"Yeah. And Johnson is rich enough to hire someone to do the murder, even if he was out of town."

"Right."

"So next step is . . . ?"

"Grill Ken again. And we need his bank records, and hers. See if there are any large payments. Comb through Johnson's background again. Maybe call in some favors at LAPD if you can. See if he's as clean as he appears."

Back at the office, Bob told Sarah to call Glick and tell him to come in tomorrow morning at 10:00 and to bring his bank statements. A few minutes later, Sarah buzzed to say Glick was on the line, saying he had plans tomorrow.

Bob picked up the phone.

"Ken, you'll be here in my office tomorrow morning at ten if you want me to remain your lawyer. And bring those bank statements."

He didn't wait for a reply.

That night, Marcus could tell Bob was upset.

"Is it the case?"

"Kenny. He's maybe not as angelic as he lets on."

"How do you mean?"

"I shouldn't say."

"Don't let it get to you. I'm sure he's upset, rattled. Really, he's a good guy. I trust him."

Bob frowned.

"Relax this weekend," Marcus added.

"I can't. I'm giving Kenny the third degree tomorrow morning. And I invited Anna and Sarah and Jason to dinner tomorrow night. Sarah is bringing her boyfriend. Brad."

"Well . . . the more the merrier. What are we cooking?"

"You're doing the shopping and setting the table. I'm making *coq au vin*."

"My cooking has improved, hasn't it?" Marcus said, looking a bit forlorn.

"Umm. I plead the Fifth."

47

Saturday morning Bob got up early to meet Kenny. He was dreading the confrontation; he hated having to confront people about their sex lives, but in a lot of his cases, he had to. Before leaving for the office he wrote out a shopping list for Marcus.

"Jason is bringing wine, and Sarah said she'd bring dessert, so we're set there."

"Okey dokey." Marcus could tell Bob was tense about meeting Kenny. He was dying to know what was going on, but didn't ask.

Jason arrived at the office a few minutes before 10:00 and put the coffee on, and Kenny arrived at 10:05. They settled in Bob's office.

"Kenny, I told you before, I can't defend you if I don't know everything."

Kenny nodded. He was nervous.

"We met with Alex Johnson yesterday."

"Yes."

"And he told us he gave you and Cathy money after your, um, your sessions."

Kenny turned bright red.

"Is that true?"

"Yes."

"Did you or Cathy ask for money in advance?"

"No!" Kenny practically shouted.

"And Johnson just offered money, when? After? As you were getting dressed?"

"Something like that."

"Did that surprise you?"

"No."

Bob and Jason looked at each other.

"Why not?"

"It's just kind of the way it worked."

"The way what worked?"

"These older men. They like sex. I mean, who doesn't? And they're well off and they offer . . . gifts. One gave Cathy a bracelet. Sometimes they offer caviar and champagne or something like that. Most just gave cash."

"And you never asked for cash in advance? Are you telling me the truth?"

"No, I never asked. And yes, that's the truth. Of course . . ."

"Yes?"

"Of course I can't be sure Cathy didn't mention cash before she saw people one-on-one."

Bob and Jason let that sink in.

"Did you bring your bank statements?"

"Yes." He reached for a folder out of his shoulder bag.

"I'll take those," Jason began looking through them.

"You realize, Ken, don't you, that what you did with these men could be construed as prostitution?"

"It wasn't like that." He was getting scared, Bob could tell.

"I'm sure the police would see it that way. This could sink us. In the eyes of the jury you'd be a criminal."

"Well let's hope they don't find out about this."

"I need to ask you something else about these sessions."

Kenny waited.

"Are you bisexual? I'm not here to judge, but I need to know."

"No, I'm not."

"So what would happen in these sessions? Sexually?"

"They were three-ways."

"So both you and the other . . . gentlemen were the active partner, and Cathy was the passive partner?"

"Yes. And sometimes the other guy just wanted to watch."

"I see."

"For how long a period of time were you and Cathy accepting these tips?"

Kenny thought for a moment. "About eighteen months."

"It was always cash? Never a check or anything like that?"

"No checks. Look, I know how this looks. But this wasn't about money."

"Then what was it about?"

"Like I said before, sex. Cathy wanting to meet a lot of people, sometimes Hollywood guys, maybe make a connection that could help her career. And if not . . ."

Kenny paused.

"And if not . . ."

"She wanted to learn more about what made people tick. How they behaved. How she'd feel doing these things. For her acting."

"And you were comfortable with that?"

"Yes, I was. We didn't do it that often. It's not like it was a major part of our life."

Bob paused, stared at him hard. "Okay. That's it for today."

Jason, who had been looking through Kenny's bank statements, said he'd finish going through them and then give them back.

Kenny left without saying anything more, while Bob got up and poured himself another cup of coffee.

"I'm not seeing any large deposits so far," Jason said. "Of course, if there was blackmail money, there could be an account somewhere else. Or cash in a safe deposit box somewhere. I can check with some of the local banks."

"Did you buy his story?" Bob asked.

"Yes. No. Maybe. I don't know."

"Neither do I. The kid is driving me crazy. I don't know what's real and what's not with him. But there's one good thing," Bob said.

"What's that?"

"The police arrested Kenny. So they probably aren't poking around, looking for this kind of thing."

"So we're glad our client was arrested."

"Yeah." Bob gave out a little laugh.

"It's interesting," Jason said, "that he left open the possibility that Cathy could have been asking for money up front. In fact, he kinda went out of his way to mention it."

"Yes, I noticed that too."

"And I hate to say this, but . . ."

"But?"

"If Cathy was seeing people alone, and taking cash, and not sharing it with Ken . . ." Jason didn't finish his sentence.

"Then he might have had motive." Bob said. He threw his pen down on his desk.

"We need her bank records."

"Yeah. I'll put in for a court order on Monday."

"Right," Jason said.

They were quiet for a minute.

"It's not uncommon, you know," Jason said.

"What?"

"Young people with older sugar daddies. I saw a lot of it when I was a detective."

"And it's not considered prostitution?"

"It's a fine line. We mostly looked at it as a victimless crime. So we left it alone. Usually."

"Well, there was a victim here. And she's dead."

48

In the early afternoon, Bob took Oscar for a long walk, hoping it would clear his head. Then he began making dinner. Cooking always soothed him.

Marcus tidied up the living room and set the table. Then they both took showers and dressed.

Jason, Anna, Sarah and Brad, a lawyer for the ACLU, all arrived around 7:00. Jason had brought several bottles of Pinot Noir, and Bob offered everyone a glass before dinner. Oscar, as usual, went up to each new person and demanded to be petted as if he had been kept in a closet for months, starved, and deprived of human touch. Anna got down on the floor to cuddle him, and he purred, almost like a kitten.

"What a beautiful dog," she said. On cue, Oscar licked her chin.

The *coq au vin* was a hit, and conversation was lively. Bob asked Brad what sort of cases he was working on at the ACLU.

"Gay and lesbian discharges from the military. There are more now, not less. Clinton's policy is a disaster."

"Ridiculous," Jason said.

"Insane," Brad replied. "I mean, anyone who has spent any time at all around here knows the Marine corps and the Navy are full of gay men. And why shouldn't they be?"

Anna asked if they have a legal chance.

"Not much. It's awfully hard to convince a jury that their superiors, these lieutenants and captains in their shiny uniforms, aren't telling the whole truth and nothing but."

Everyone was quiet for a moment.

"I'd really like to show Clinton the lives he's ruining," Brad went on. "Not to mention Rwanda. Where the hell were we? We care about human rights except when it actually matters? That was genocide, pure and simple."

"Yeah, that bothers me too," Bob said.

"I don't think the guy cares about much beyond the bond market," Brad said with a disgusted tone.

The conversation reminded Marcus of what Kenny thought about Clinton—mostly style, not much substance. You could certainly make an argument that his talk about human rights and his "Don't Ask, Don't Tell" policy for gays in the military were for show. The realities were something else.

Gloom was settling over the table, so Bob announced that Anna had brought flan for dessert. He and Marcus went into the kitchen to get it ready and to make coffee and tea. They served it with an old port they had been saving for a special occasion.

"Do you do any work on immigration?" Anna asked Brad.

"We do, or I should say, the office does, but it's not my specialty. Is that what you're mostly interested in?"

"I'm not sure. But yes, maybe."

"Well, if Bob mistreats you, come see me."

"Hey, no poaching," Bob said to general laughter.

The party broke up around 10:00. Anna offered to stay and help with the dishes, but Bob shooed her away. While they were cleaning up, Marcus said "She's really nice."

"Yeah, she is. And smart."

"You'd like to do some immigration work, right?"

"I've thought about it. In fact I've had fantasies that if Anna works out, she could join the office as an associate. We could take more cases, including immigration. Assuming I can afford to pay her a real salary. We'd have to increase our case load."

"We could use some of the Kandinsky money. For a while. While you expanded."

"Um. Maybe. But we need that money for when you're old and decrepit."

"I beg your pardon. And what about when you're old and decrepit?"

"Me? I've decided to stay thirty-one forever."

"Ohhhhhh."

49

On Sunday, they slept late, or as late as Oscar would let them, and Bob made brunch, a huge mushroom omelet, which they ate out on the patio while reading the Sunday newspapers. Marcus had papers to grade and a lecture to prepare, so Bob went to the office to look over his notes about various cases.

His mind kept wandering back to Kenny. Was he innocent?

Merely young and foolish and sexually adventurous? Or could he have done the murder?

The circumstances did point to him. He admits they spent the night together. Apparently their relationship was volatile.

But then, what young relationship wasn't? Until he met Marcus, he had several boyfriends with whom he ended up in terrible fights. One even threw a glass pitcher at him, which he ducked; it hit the wall and shattered. Bob walked out and never saw him again.

And the older men and money angle. That was disturbing. But the state case for murder was still weak.

"Reasonable doubt, Bobby," he said out loud.

He wanted to talk the case over with his father but didn't want to bother him. He dialed Danbury and talked to his mother; she sounded like her old self, which was reassuring. Then she put Jake on the phone.

"Don't let her overdo it," Bob said. "She needs to rest."

"When have you ever known your mother to sit still?"

Bob could hear his mother say "I heard that" in the distance, probably from the kitchen.

He smiled and said goodbye.

That night they went to their favorite restaurant for dinner, California Cuisine in Hillcrest, where they sat at a table on the patio. After dinner, they wandered along University Avenue, stopping in the gay bookstore, and then drove to an ice cream parlor in Kensington, where they ran into Fred Taylor, an academic colleague of Marcus's, someone he usually tried to avoid. He was alone and he invited them to sit at his table, and, since the place was crowded, there was nowhere else to sit. They didn't want to seem rude, so they did.

As they ate their ice cream, Taylor began his usual monologue of who was up and who was down on campus, who published in what journal, who was invited to speak where, who might get an offer from Stanford and who might be the next chancellor.

Like most of the faculty at UCSD, he had the ability to talk without taking a breath, oblivious to everyone around them.

When they left and got out onto the sidewalk, Marcus sighed. "And that," he told Bob, "is why I'm beginning to hate the place. It's like high school on steroids."

50

The work week that began the following day was the week the world learned that O.J. Simpson had almost certainly murdered his ex-wife and a waiter friend of hers, who had returned the sunglasses she had left behind at a restaurant. On Monday the murders hit the news, and later in the week, the globe was glued to television screens watching a live, low-speed chase of Simpson down Los Angeles freeways. In the months that followed, television became all O.J., all the time.

For Bob, the Simpson melodrama made him think harder about whether Kenny did in fact have a motive for killing Cathy Yaeger. Maybe, as it seemed with O.J., it was an argument that got way out of hand or a case of jealous rage. Maybe Cathy was seeing someone else—apart from the older men—or beginning to cool on their relationship. Maybe Cathy was withholding cash from her trysts. Or maybe it was a rough sex session that went too far, especially given the drug and alcohol in her system.

All seemed possible. And Bob was always suspicious of clients out of whom he had to drag information, bit by bit.

Or maybe Alex Johnson had Cathy killed because she and

Kenny were blackmailing him, threatening to expose him. His wife may have known about his affairs, but the public certainly didn't, and the risk of that exposure would have been too great for a family like the Cunninghams to contemplate, pillars of society that they were.

By midweek, they had acquired Cathy's bank records, and Jason and Anna were pouring through them.

"There's a large deposit of $10,000," Jason announced on Wednesday afternoon.

Bob closed his eyes. "From when?"

"About six weeks before she died."

"It could have an innocent explanation," Bob said, though he doubted his own words. "Maybe an old aunt died, left it to her. Something like that."

"Or . . ." Jason didn't finish his sentence.

"Yes. Or."

"Can you trace the origin of the deposit?"

"I already tried. The bank is tight-lipped, they always are, but I did find out it was a check drawn on a Los Angeles bank."

"Okay. So we need to set up another meeting with her parents, see if they know anything. And where are we on Cunningham?"

"He's agreed to see us Saturday morning at his beach house."

"And what about driving Kenny around to houses he and Cathy visited? Other trysts."

Bob didn't know what else to call them. The police would no doubt call them tricks.

"We've done a bit of that already. I've gotten some names, addresses. You want me to push him on this? He always seems to have a reason he's too busy to do this."

"Definitely. When you get the names, check their records,

backgrounds. Put together a file. And ask Sarah to see if she can set up another meeting with Cathy's parents."

"Copy that."

Bob spent the rest of the week working on other cases with Anna, who impressed him more and more.

On Thursday, Ruth had her first radiation treatment. Bob called that evening and spoke to his father.

"It was pretty bad," Jake said. "Worse than the chemo, but the doctor told us to expect that. Lots of throwing up. She's asleep now, finally."

"Do you want me to fly out?"

"I don't think she wants you boys to see her like this. I told Alex the same thing. Maybe when this is over. She may let Carol come in the meantime. You know, woman-to-woman kind of thing."

"How many more treatments?"

"Two."

"Oh, God."

"She's trying to be cheerful. But I think this is getting to her."

"And what about you?"

"Oh, you know . . ."

"I know, one foot in front of the other."

"On the bright side, I'm learning how to cook. I'm almost as good as Marcus."

"In that case, you're both going to lose weight."

Jake laughed.

When he got off the phone, Bob went outside for some fresh air. In all his thirty-one years, he had never known his mother to be anything less than cheerful, happy, active. He wished he could be there but he understood why she wouldn't want him there.

He felt helpless, and far away.

He went back inside and tried to concentrate on work. Anna could tell he was upset.

"Is it your mom?"

"Yeah. Radiation treatments."

"Those can be really hard on the body, I know. But if it prevents the cancer from coming back . . ."

"Yes, you're right." Bob smiled. "Back to work."

51

On Friday, Bob and Jason met with Cathy's parents in Laguna Beach, and asked about the $10,000 deposit into her account.

"Yes, it's from us. We're supporting her through college," her father said.

"The other deposits seem to be for smaller amounts," Jason said. "Why was this one so large?"

"I'm not sure. She asked if we could make a larger deposit this time."

"And she didn't say what she needed the money for?"

"No, she didn't." Her father turned toward his wife. "Did she give you a reason?"

"Yes," Mrs. Yaeger said, looking down. Her husband looked at her with surprise.

"She said she might need to go away for a while, over the summer."

"Did she say why?" Bob asked.

"I asked, but she didn't want to say. I thought maybe . . ."

"Yes?" Bob said.

"I thought maybe she wanted a break from Kenny, maybe just for a while. Maybe to think over the relationship."

Bob and Jason let that sink in.

"Did she say anything along those lines?"

"No. Just a hunch. Call it mother's intuition."

Mr. Yaeger stood up. He was clearly pissed off at his wife. "Is there anything else?"

"No," Bob said. "Thank you for seeing us."

"You know the way out."

"Well," Jason said, back in the car.

"Yes."

"Motive."

"If it's true. She didn't know for sure. Pull off the freeway, I want to find a phone."

Bob called Sarah, asked him to have Kenny in the office in an hour. "Don't take no for an answer."

He was waiting in the outer office when they got back.

"What's up?" he asked, trying but failing to sound nonchalant as they went into Bob's office.

"Kenny, I need you to tell me the truth. Cathy received a large sum of money, $10,000, from her parents, about six weeks before she died. It was much larger than their previous deposits. Do you have any idea why she needed a large sum?"

"Well, she did talk about going to France."

"Oh?"

"A friend of hers had just moved there, taken a job as an *au pair* for a family in Paris."

"Did Cathy say when she would go or for how long?"

"No. It was all kinda vague. She thought she might go for a couple of months."

"I see. And you wouldn't have gone with her?"

"No. I mean, I wanted, but I couldn't afford it, and I've

got school. She was talking about going early in the fall. And now. . . . And now there's my trial," he said with a little laugh. "Unless you can get them to drop the case."

"Well, stranger things have happened. We're chipping away at the state's evidence."

"I see."

After he left, Jason looked at Bob with his "I suspect our client isn't so innocent" look.

"I know, I know. If she was leaving him. Motive."

52

That night when Bob got home, Marcus was out with Oscar. When they got back, Oscar rushed in, full of sand, getting it all over.

"How was the beach, hmm?" Bob asked him. Oscar let out a little yip.

"God, you look awful. Hard day? Is it Kenny?" Bob asked.

"Yeah."

"Don't tell me. Probably better if I don't know."

Bob nodded.

"What should we do about dinner?"

"Pizza."

"Okay, I'll order. Mushroom and onion? Sausage?"

"Whatever you feel like."

While Marcus ordered and then fed Oscar, Bob set the table and opened a bottle of good Chianti, ideal for the pizza. Bob drank most of it. Marcus was beginning to worry a bit about Bob's drinking; there had been a definite uptick in the last few weeks. He knew he was worried about Ruth, and that Kenny's case was getting to him; he wished he knew how to help.

"What if, after Ruth's last treatment, we visit and then go up to Provincetown for a week? Or Miller's Cove?" Miller's Cove was the little beach resort in Maine where they had met, ten years before.

"That's a great idea. Assuming I can get away. And that Mom is okay."

Bob worked on other cases until Saturday, when it was time for the interview with James Cunningham. He dreaded it. Cunningham was devious and slippery.

He drove up to Cunningham's beach house with Jason for their 2:00 meeting. Bob seemed sullen on the way up.

"You really don't like this guy, huh?" Jason asked.

"No, I don't. And I don't trust him."

Cunningham himself opened the door, wearing sandals and a linen shirt and slacks.

"Counselor, what a pleasure. Come in. And who is your handsome sidekick?"

Bob introduced Jason, and they shook hands.

Cunningham had a glass in his hand; the contents smelled like brandy.

"Can I offer you anything? Coffee? Tea? A soft drink?"

They both said they were fine, and the three of them settled in the living room. The glass doors to the deck overlooking the Pacific were open, and the smell of the ocean was almost overpowering. Cunningham arranged himself on one of the white couches in a provocative pose, arms outstretched.

"So, how can I help you?"

Bob spoke. "We understand that you were acquainted with Catherine Yaeger before her death."

"Yes, I knew her. Quite tragic."

"Did you also know Kenneth Glick?"

"I did." He took a sip of his drink.

"How did you meet them?"

"It was quite by accident, at the Old Globe. Some dreary Shakespeare, as I remember. During intermission, out in front of the theater. They were talking about the play. I was standing near them, then said something in response to something Catherine said. I don't remember what. We chatted."

"And how did the relationship proceed?"

"When it was time to go back in, I offered them my card, suggesting they come over next time I was down here."

Cunningham's main residence, Bob knew, was in Los Angeles.

"And they called?"

"Kenny did, yes."

"And how did things proceed?"

"Well, I was going to be back down here the following week, this was last summer, and I invited them to dinner."

"Here?"

"Yes, here. They came, and after dinner we got into the hot tub."

"And?"

"And after a while, I suggested we move inside."

"Go on, please."

"I invited them to stay."

Bob dreaded the next question.

"Did either of them mention money?"

"Yes. Catherine did. She said something along the lines of they're both being poor students."

"And you understood that to mean . . ."

"That they expected compensation. Which I provided. Gladly."

"How many times did you see them?"

"A few. Perhaps four or five?"

"Always together?"

"No. Together once more, as I recall. And then Catherine alone a few times. Perhaps it added up to more than five."

"And was compensation provided each time?"

"Yes."

"How much?"

"As I recall, it was $500 each time."

"Always in cash?"

"Yes."

Cunningham got up, went to a bar, and refilled his glass.

"And how would you characterize your intimacy?"

"It was delightful."

"Would you call it rough?" Jason asked.

"I wouldn't, but I suppose some would."

"Did you get a sense of the relationship between the two of them?"

"They seemed in sync."

"Meaning?"

"I got the impression this was not a new thing for them, if you know what I mean." He sipped.

"Did you ever see Mr. Glick alone?"

"Once, with another female friend of mine."

"On that occasion, did he say anything about money?"

"No. It was understood."

"And you gave their names to Alex Johnson?"

"Yes, I did."

"Even though Mr. Johnson was married to your mother?" Bob asked.

"Come now, counselor. Let's not be naïve."

"Was this your first . . ." Bob searched for the right word, "referral to Mr. Johnson?"

"No."

"Did you notice any tension between Ms. Yaeger and Mr. Glick?" Jason asked.

"Well, not exactly. But I got the impression Ms. Yaeger was in charge. Of course, that could have been part of their performance."

"And you're sure she was the one who solicited funds, so to speak?"

"Yes. Quite sure."

"Were you surprised when you heard that Mr. Glick was arrested for Ms. Yaeger's murder?"

"I couldn't really say, either way. One never knows what people are capable if, does one?"

Bob glanced at Jason, as if to say, can you think of anything else to ask.

Cunningham broke the silence. "Will I be called upon to testify? Obviously, I would prefer not to."

"I can't say at this point. But this is a case of murder."

"I understand. In that case, if we need to speak again, please contact my attorney. You remember him from our last murder, I assume?"

"Yes, I do. Thank you for your time."

"Not at all."

Driving back, Jason said, "That is one cool customer."

Bob smirked. "That's one word for it."

"Legally speaking, did Yaeger solicit? Would a jury say so?"

"It's a bit murky. But less murky than it was before. It's pretty clear they knew what they were doing."

"Interesting," Jason said, "that it was Yaeger who mentioned money."

"Yes, it is. If Cunningham can be believed."

"So back to Glick?"

"Back to Glick."

Bob was getting really tired of prying information out of his client.

53

On Monday Bob was in court on another case, so he did not meet with Kenny again until Tuesday afternoon.

"Kenny, I am going to drop you as a client unless you start telling me the truth. The whole truth."

Kenny was silent as Bob recounted the conversation with Cunningham.

"Is he telling the truth?"

Kenny looked down. "Yes."

"Did you know Cathy was going to ask for money?"

"This wasn't the first time. But I never really knew when she was going to and when she wasn't."

"When was the first?"

He thought for a moment. "Honestly, I don't remember."

"Did she discuss it with you in advance?"

"No. Once I asked her why she did it. And she said she wanted to know what it felt like, for her acting."

"And when you saw these same people alone, did you solicit funds?"

"No!"

"But you didn't turn them down."

"No."

"When you did these visits together, did you split the money?"

"Yes."

"Fifty-fifty?"

"Yes."

"Kenny, do you realize that if the police learn about this, as they well might, you could be charged with another crime? This is America. We don't like sex for money."

Kenny didn't respond. He looked down.

"And that the prosecutor in your case could say this was a motive that led you to murder?"

Kenny was now in a panic. "A motive? How?"

"Maybe Cathy cut you out of the take. At a minimum, this doesn't exactly make you look like an innocent young graduate student."

"Look," Kenny said, speaking very firmly. "I did not kill Cathy. Maybe what we did was stupid. Wrong. But it really was just for fun, and a little extra cash. Why would I kill her?"

"Have the police contacted you since you were released on bail?"

"No. I would have told you."

"Well that's good."

There was a long pause.

"Are you going to drop my case?"

"Not yet. But if there are any more surprises, I will. Do you understand?"

"Yes."

"So tell me now, if there is anything else I need to know."

"There isn't."

Bob decided to ask a question that would throw him off.

"Oh? Did Cathy ever use shackles during these scenes? Or when she was with you, one-on-one?"

"Not when I was there. But I knew she did sometimes

use them when I wasn't. Some guys . . ."

"Yes?"

"Some guys just like that. For the woman to be in charge. It was just . . ."

"Just?"

"Just a kind of performance."

Bob turned to Jason, who had been sitting in, taking notes.

"Where are you on finding the names of other guys? The scouting trips?"

Jason looked at Kenny. "We've gotten a few."

"Are there more?" Bob asked Jason.

"A few I can remember."

"Get to it, please," Bob said to both of them, and they both nodded.

54

After Kenny left, Jason came back into Bob's office. "So?" he asked.

"So. This is now pretty clear solicitation. If the police get hold of this, we could be sunk with a jury, unless we find clear evidence of innocence, or can prove someone else killed her."

"Which means . . ."

"If the police do find this out, I would urge Kenny to take a plea."

"Will the police find out?"

Bob thought for a moment. "Hard to say. They haven't

yet. If they had, they would have brought him in for more questioning, or taken depositions. I need to find out if they have. I'll ask for a pre-trial conference."

Jason nodded.

"Who are the guys you've found so far?"

"A few Hollywood types. Forty- to fiftyish, executive types."

"Well that strengthens the case for Cathy's motive being her career. That's something. We'll need to interview those guys."

"Do you want Sarah to set them up?"

"Not yet. Marcus and I may go away for a bit after the Fourth. But keep driving around with Kenny, and push him to be thorough."

"Are we required to turn this information over to the prosecution?"

"Under California law, only if there were written statements or tapes, which we won't create."

Jason nodded.

"Do you think he's innocent?"

"At this point, I have no idea."

"There's something that bothers me," Jason said.

Bob waited.

"What her mother said. About her wanting to get away from him. France."

"Yeah, that bothers me too. Although . . ."

"Although?"

"It's clear they were both operators. Yaeger may have just wanted or needed the money. What she told her mother could have been a cover story."

"Right. I hadn't thought of that. What a mess."

Bob sighed. "Murder always is."

55

The next day, Sarah buzzed him to say Melinda Ivanov was on the phone.

"Melinda. How are you?"

"I'm all right. Back in town. I'll be glad to take a look at those autopsy photos now."

"Thank you. I'll have them messengered over. Is your father . . ."

"Yes. He's gone. Honestly, it was a blessing. He was suffering."

"I'm so sorry."

"Thank you. We can talk or meet once I've seen the photos."

Two days later, she called back. Bob invited her to dinner at his house for the following evening.

When she arrived, Bob could see that her father's ordeal had taken a toll; she looked exhausted. Bob introduced Marcus. It was a warm evening so they ate out on the patio, *coq au vin* again. After dinner Marcus cleared the table and then excused himself, knowing they had business to discuss.

Over coffee, Melinda said she had gone over the photos and her assistant's autopsy report, as well as the photos from the second autopsy.

"Goldstein is adamant that the bruising was not there during his autopsy. His photos do not show it. I would say the bruising is relatively minor, and was twenty-four to seventy-two hours old. It was not the cause of death. I concur with Robert, she died as a result of a fatal mixture of Demerol and alcohol. Given her weight, which was slight, the amounts of both in her system were rather extreme. And reckless."

"And you would testify to this in court?"

"Yes, absolutely."

"Thank you. That's very helpful."

"Not at all. I really resent that the police are portraying Robert as incompetent. He is anything but."

"Have you ever seen the police mischaracterize the cause of death as a tactic? To try to force a plea bargain?"

Melinda needed to be careful, which Bob understood.

"Let's just say it's not unheard of."

Bob smiled. "Again, thanks," he said. "This is incredibly helpful."

"To tell you the truth, I'm getting really tired of the politics in this job. I may retire soon. You were smart to leave the DA when you did."

"Well, solo practice has its downside too."

She smiled. "I'm sure."

Melinda stood up. "Thank you for a lovely dinner."

Bob walked her inside and to the door, and Marcus came out to say goodbye. Bob wanted to hug her, but he didn't think she would find that appropriate.

"Was she a help? Marcus asked.

"Yes. Definitely."

Bob looked more relaxed than Marcus had seen him for a while.

56

The next day Bob requested a pre-trial meeting in front of the new judge in Superior Court, Sally Murphy, which was quickly arranged for the next morning, a Friday, at 8:00 a.m. Bob knew nothing about this judge; he had never even heard of her. *Must be a new appointment*, he thought. That could be good or bad, he knew; good if she were unsure of herself, which could mean she'd make mistakes that would be useful on appeal; bad, however, if she hoped to quickly establish a reputation as hard-nosed.

"Eight sharp," the judge's clerk said.

Bob dressed carefully and arrived on time, as did Billy Lewis. They walked into the judge's chambers together.

"So, gentlemen, what's on your mind?"

"Your Honor," Bob said, "I'd like to make sure the prosecution has complied with discovery, and turned over any and all transcripts of witness statements."

"We have," Billy said simply.

"In that case, Your Honor, I believe the prosecution's case is exceedingly weak and should be dismissed."

It was a ploy that Bob knew wouldn't work, but it never hurt to plant a seed of doubt in the judge's mind.

"Nice try, counselor. Denied. Is there anything else?"

Both of them shook their heads.

"There is one thing from my end," the judge said. "I'm glad you're both here. My schedule has been shifting around, and it turns out they need to do some renovations in the building. Earthquake mitigation. I need to push the trial date to November 6. Any objections?"

"No, Your Honor," they both said simultaneously.

"In that case, thank you for coming in. Next time, you might perhaps come with something real."

Bob and Billy walked out together.

"Nice try," Billy said.

"Your case is weak, Billy, and getting weaker. I've already successfully challenged the testimony of one of your key witnesses, Rebecca Morrison. You have the transcript. She doesn't know what she saw or heard that night. You've not shown a motive. Melinda is back, and she'll testify that it was drugs and booze that killed the victim."

"We'll see, counselor. Have a good day." And with that, Billy left the building.

Bob smiled. He liked Billy, despite being on opposite sides, and knew it was almost certainly Fred Stevens, the DA, pushing for a trial and conviction.

Bob spent the rest of the day working on a brief for another case with Anna, who had done a first draft. It was excellent. Bob hardly had to make any changes.

"Anna," he said on an impulse, "after this year, I'd be interested in hiring you as an associate. We'd be able to expand the practice to immigration cases, which I've not done so far. If you're interested. Think about it."

"Yes! Yes! That would be wonderful," she said.

"Think about it, though. I'm sure you could get a job with many of the firms in town, and they'd be able to pay you more than I could."

"Yes, and they'd stick me with boring cases and background research. I'd never get into court."

Bob empathized. When he'd finished law school, he, too, was eager to get to real lawyering.

"Well, think about it. Explore your options. We'll talk about it again."

Anna thanked him and, to his surprise, gave him a kiss on the cheek.

That evening, Marcus and Bob went to the opening of *Street Theater* at Diversionary, the play about Stonewall. It was a great production with a big cast, full of laughs, and the opening night crowd loved it. After the performance they went to the cast party at Andy Rich's apartment.

Bob seemed more relaxed than he had for a long time, and Marcus noticed.

Beth, the friend of Cathy Yaeger's who had given Bob a lot of information, came up to say hello.

"You were great," Marcus said.

"Thanks. It's a fun show. I just wish . . ."

"That Cathy could have been in it?" Bob said. "I know."

"Yes. She would have been terrific."

"I'm sure."

"Are you getting anywhere in the case?" Beth asked as she sipped from a plastic cup of white wine.

"I'm not sure. Maybe. At this point, it's not clear what will happen."

"Well, thanks for coming tonight."

"Of course. We really enjoyed the play."

In the car on the way home, Marcus asked Bob if it was true that he didn't know what would happen.

"Yeah, it is. But it's early. We're still investigating. We might catch a break."

Marcus wanted to pump him for more information, but knew he shouldn't.

Bob changed the subject.

"Let's see if we can get a reservation in Miller's Cove. Anytime in July or early August."

Marcus smiled. "Sure. I'll start calling around tomorrow."

57

Bob and Jason spent the few days before the Fourth of July interviewing the two other prosecution witnesses whose depositions they had been shown, Maureen Freeman and Jane Masters.

Maureen lived in a dorm on the UCSD campus; they borrowed Marcus's office so that they could speak in private. When she walked in, Bob had to suppress a smile; another young Californian dressed as if she lived in Seattle, heavy corduroy shirt and jeans, despite the fact that it was 80-plus degrees outside.

After introductions and an explanation of why they were meeting in a faculty office, Bob began.

"Ms. Freeman, you stated in your deposition that you saw Mr. Glick 'shake' Ms. Yaeger."

"Yes."

"You said this was at a party. Whose party?"

"Um, I don't remember."

"Do you remember when this was? Or where?"

"Not really, no." She fidgeted with her knapsack.

"Do you remember *approximately* when this might have been?"

"Are you calling me a liar?" She suddenly seemed angry.

"No, not at all. But it's important we nail down the evidence as carefully as we can."

Freeman seemed to calm down. Bob treaded carefully.

"Can you describe exactly what you mean by 'shake'?"

"I just remember Kenny had his hands on Cathy and it looked like he was shaking her."

"Where exactly were his hands?"

"Um, around her waist, maybe."

"But you're not sure?"

"Um. Maybe on her shoulders."

"Had they been dancing, perhaps? Were people dancing at this party?"

She thought for a moment. "Yes, there was music, and some people were dancing."

"Is it possible that's what you saw? Dancing?"

"I don't think so. But . . ."

"But?"

There was a long pause.

"I don't know. Maybe they were dancing."

"But you don't remember where this took place?"

"No. I mean, there are a lot of parties on campus. Every weekend, you know?"

"Could you see Ms. Yaeger's face while this incident was happening?"

"Yes."

"What was her expression?"

"Normal, I guess. Whatever."

"Did she push Mr. Glick's hands away, or try to break free?"

"I don't think so."

"Did they stay at the party, together?"

"Yeah."

"Had you had anything to drink at that party?"

"Um, yeah. I had a couple of glasses of beer. There was a keg."

"I see. Did Ms. Yaeger ever talk to you about Mr. Glick?"

"Not really. She once called him 'my boyfriend.' That's about it."

"Had you ever spoken to Mr. Glick?"

"No. But I had seen him around."

"Ms. Freeman, you'll be called to testify at Mr. Glick's trial. You will be under oath, on penalty of perjury. That is a very serious matter. Are you certain you saw Mr. Glick shake Ms. Yaeger?"

Freeman looked out the window, toward the ocean. "I'm not a hundred percent sure, no."

"I see. Thank you for being honest about this."

"I mean, when the police questioned me, they were really pushing. I had never talked to the police before. I was nervous. Really nervous and upset."

"That's perfectly understandable."

"Do you have any idea why the police questioned you?"

"I think because Cathy and I had a couple of classes together that semester. Her last semester, I mean."

Bob gave her his card. "If you do remember anything more about the incident, could you give me a call?"

"Yeah, sure."

"Thanks again."

And with that, she quickly left the office.

Bob looked at Jason, who was shaking his head.

"Worthless. Or close to it," Jason said.

"No kidding."

That afternoon, back at the office, Bob called Kenny. Jason was there and he put Kenny on speaker.

"Kenny, do you know Maureen Freeman?"

"Maureen. Freeman. Short brown hair, blue eyes, around five foot three? Dressed in grunge?"

"Yes." Bob smiled. *So that's what it's called. Grunge-wear.*

"Yeah. She was in a section I taught. Intro to American Politics, I think it was. I definitely had the feeling she was coming on to me." Jason looked bewildered, so he added, "Everyone in the grad program teaches discussion sections."

"Would you have a record of the class?"

"Yeah, sure. I have the class list, I'm sure, or can get it. It's all computerized."

"Do you remember if she got a decent grade?"

"She didn't. She got a C. You have to be pretty bad to get a C in an intro course as UCSD."

"Okay, thanks." They hung up.

Bob and Jason both guffawed.

"So," Jason said, "you introduce the class list at the trial, after questioning her, and . . ."

"Assuming she sticks to what she told us, she loses all credibility with the jury. Not that there was much to begin with."

That night, Bob asked Marcus why so many kids in their twenties dressed they way they did.

"It's the Kurt Cobain effect."

Bob had no idea who that was, but was too tired to ask.

58

The next day, Jane Masters volunteered to come to Bob's office after work; she had a summer internship nearby. In the morning, Bob called Kenny again and asked if her name rang a bell.

"Oh yeah, definitely. We dated for a while."

"When was this?"

"Um, it was just before I met Cathy. Right after I got to UCSD. So three years ago."

"And what happened?"

"We didn't really click," Kenny said simply.

"Who ended it?"

"I did, after a few months."

"Was she upset?"

"Well, yeah, I'd say so. She cried."

"Okay, thanks."

Masters arrived at 5:30. She was an attractive blonde and looked more mature than her age. If he had passed her on the street, Bob would have guessed she was in her early thirties. She was dressed for work in a skirt, blouse, high heels. A career woman in the making. *Maybe even a lawyer*, he thought.

He thanked her for coming in. She nodded.

"Ms. Masters, you said in your deposition that Mr. Glick drank heavily."

"Yes."

"On what basis did you make that statement?"

"We knew each other. We briefly dated. And we went to some parties together. On campus."

"And how would you define 'heavy' drinking?"

"Well, two or three drinks at a time. Pretty much every time I saw him."

"And what would Mr. Glick be drinking?"

"It varied. Scotch, vodka. Beer. Sometimes tequila. And he'd mix them."

"Would he become inebriated? Loud? Aggressive?"

"Well, no. Not really."

"Did you ever feel unsafe with Mr. Glick after he drank, for example, driving?"

"Um, no."

"Did he ever strike you?"

"No." She looked down at her purse in her lap.

"You also stated that Mr. Glick 'wanted' Catherine Yaeger to drink. On what basis did you make that statement?"

"I saw them together. When Ken would get a drink for himself, he would get one for Cathy."

"Did Cathy willingly accept these drinks?"

She thought for a moment. "I couldn't say either way."

"When you dated, did Mr. Glick want you to drink more than you yourself wanted?"

"I usually had one drink."

"And?"

"Kenny would ask if I wanted another."

"He would ask?"

"Yes."

"And then?"

"I would say no."

"And then?"

"And then he'd get one or two more for himself."

"Did that ever cause an argument?"

"No, not really."

"So, in other words, he accepted that you would drink less?"

"Yes." Masters was getting flustered.

"Did you ever see an argument with Ms. Yaeger about these drinks?"

"Well, no."

"Did she ever speak to you about this?"

"No, she didn't."

"How did your relationship with Mr. Glick end?"

Her demeanor changed. "He ended it."

"Did that upset you?"

"Well, yes. No one likes being dumped."

Bob smiled. "True. Well, thank you for coming in."

"Will I need to testify at the trial?"

"Hard to say at the moment. It's possible. Just tell the truth, straight-forwardly, as you have today. Here is my card. If you remember anything else you think might be relevant, please contact me."

The next morning, Jason asked Bob how the interview

with Masters had gone; he had had an appointment he couldn't miss and hadn't been there.

"This may be the weakest case for murder in the history of California. These witnesses are useless."

59

It was now early July. Marcus and Bob planned to fly to Danbury, spend a few days, and then drive up to Miller's Cove. Marcus had managed somehow to snag a reservation at a B&B they had stayed in several times years before.

"Lucky timing," Marcus had said. "They had just had a cancellation when I called."

Carol had already visited to help Ruth and Jake through the remaining radiation treatments; she, Alex, and Jay were planning to visit later in July.

Marcus and Bob took Oscar to the kennel, which always made them feel like they were committing a felony. But the nice thing about the kennel, north of San Diego, was that it had vast open spaces and let the dogs play freely. In the car Oscar always looked like he knew where they were going, and gave them a pitiful look, but as soon as they arrived he wagged his tail, greeted the owner, and was off with the other dogs.

"He's very popular," the owner had once said. "It's a good thing he's fixed."

The next day they flew to JFK, rented a car, and arrived in Danbury in the evening.

Jake greeted them, hugging them both. Ruth was in the den, dozing under a blanket that had been Bob's when he was a boy.

They were shocked by her appearance and tried not to show it. Ruth looked like she had aged five years. Her skin was pale and her hair was limp. She got up, which they could see was not easy for her.

"Boys," she said, hugging them both.

They all sat.

"How was your trip?" Ruth asked.

"Oh, fine, fine. Long."

Ruth laughed, which made her cough a bit.

"How do you feel?" Bob asked, as gently as he could.

"A little better every day. The doctor says I'm doing well. But I wouldn't recommend radiation treatment, even for Cousin Gert."

Bob laughed. Gert was a pretentious snob who lived in Manhattan, and the only person he could remember his mother saying she disliked. They had grown up together and been friends, but then Gert went to Radcliffe and, as his mother once put it, decided she was a Yankee blueblood who must have somehow been adopted by a Jewish family.

"Come into the kitchen. You must be hungry. Airplane food is so awful."

"Almost as bad as my cooking," Marcus said, which made everyone smile.

Ruth sat with Marcus at the kitchen table while Jake and Bob got plates and raided the fridge, coming back with cold chicken and coleslaw and iced tea.

They chatted about this and that, and then Ruth announced she was going to bed. She kissed them both and said she'd see them in the morning.

After she had gone up, Bob turned to Jake.

"I know," Jake said. "She doesn't look well. But the doctors say it's to be expected after two surgeries and radiation.

She is getting stronger."

Bob's eyes were moist. Marcus didn't know what to say.

Jake went up after a while. Still on California time, Marcus and Bob stayed up a bit longer.

Upstairs, Bob collapsed on his old bed.

"Give it time," Marcus said. "The important thing is that they got the cancer." He didn't know what else to say.

Bob didn't respond. He turned away, toward the window. Finally he got up, got undressed, and took a shower. He said nothing more before finally falling asleep.

60

The next morning, when Bob woke up, Marcus's bed was empty, and he heard voices from the kitchen. He went to the bathroom, put on a robe, and went down.

Marcus was making French toast and telling Ruth and Jake about some of the crazy things his students said or did.

"I once asked them on a quiz to name all the states that touched Illinois, just to see if they knew," Marcus was saying. He had grown up in Chicago. "You wouldn't believe what some of them said. New York. Mississippi. Arkansas."

Ruth looked a bit more like her old self, and was laughing.

"California," Bob said, "getting himself a cup of coffee. It's a different country."

"Then," Marcus went on, "I asked them to name an American who had won a Nobel prize or the National Book Award or a Pulitzer. No one had a name. Not one."

Jake shook his head.

After breakfast Jake went to his home office to make

some calls, and the others took their coffee out to the garden. It was looking a bit neglected, although the roses were blooming and smelled sweet.

"I know," Ruth said, "the yard needs work. Your father wants to hire someone."

"We can work on it while we're here," Bob said, and later than morning, they started. Marcus knew it would be good for Bob to keep busy. They pulled weeds, cut the grass, pruned the roses. It was a nice day but felt muggy; they both had gotten used to the lower humidity in San Diego and the crisp breeze there from the ocean. They sweated.

For lunch Ruth made borscht, Bob's favorite, and served it with thick black bread from a local bakery Bob remembered. They ate out on the patio. In the afternoon Ruth took a nap, Jake went to his office, and Marcus and Bob visited Claudia, one of his oldest friends, now married, still in Danbury, and taking care of young twins.

"I can hardly believe they're yours," Bob said, as the two little boys smiled up at him from their playpen.

"Oh, they're mine all right, and I've got the scars to prove it."

Bob laughed.

"So," Claudia said, "how's solo practice?"

"It has its ups and downs. But it's nice not having a boss."

Claudia had done a year of law school but dropped out to get married. She had meant to go back, but, as she had said more than once, one thing led to another.

Back home, they ordered Chinese take-out for dinner. Ruth again went to bed early and Marcus and Bob sat in the den with Jake, drinking white wine spritzers.

"I'm thinking of retiring fairly soon," Jake said.

"Really?" Bob said, taken aback. It was hard to imagine

his father not working.

"In a year or two. And we've talked about moving out to California. Maybe Palm Springs."

"Wow," Bob said.

"I mean, it kind of makes sense. You guys are there, your brother and Carol and Jay are there, and Carol says they're thinking about another baby."

That was news. Marcus could see that Bob was trying to absorb it all.

"And we'd be glad to get away from winter. Maybe we'd buy a small condo here, come back in the fall or spring, see old friends."

"Have you even been to Palm Springs?" Bob asked.

"Yes, once or twice, when you boys were tiny. It's beautiful."

"It is. But wicked hot in the summer," Marcus said.

"Well, so a house with a pool," Jake said, smiling. "And I could learn to play golf."

"Oh, I'd like to see that," Bob said. "You in green pants."

"Or maybe Laguna Beach," Jake went on. "Halfway between you and your brother."

"Now that would be nice," Bob said.

"We're just at the thinking-about-it stage. Nothing definite."

"Does Mom like the idea?"

"Actually she brought it up."

"Oh." After a pause he added, "Wow."

When they went to bed, Marcus asked Bob how he felt about what Jake had said.

"I don't know. I mean, it would be great in many ways. No more flying across the country. We'd be near if . . ."

Marcus finished the sentence. ". . . if anything happened."

"Yeah."

"Would it . . . be okay? With you, I mean," Bob asked.

"Of course," Marcus said, taking Bob's hand. "I love your folks. You know that."

Bob nodded and looked relieved.

After they both showered, Bob said, "Laguna is a better idea than Palm Springs," as he drifted off to sleep.

They spent the next few days talking over the idea with both Ruth and Jake, and they all warmed to the idea of Laguna Beach. Bob and Marcus did more gardening, and cooking, and then it was time to leave for Maine. Bob didn't really want to leave, but he didn't want to hover. They said goodbye after breakfast, and Ruth gave them a batch of chocolate chip cookies she had baked.

That made Bob smile.

"It was lovely to see you. And don't worry about me," Ruth said. "I'll be my old self in no time. I know I look like something out of a horror movie."

"No, not that bad," Bob said. "Mary Tyler Moore on a bad hair day."

"I don't think Mary has bad hair days," Marcus said, which Ruth found hilarious. She kissed them both.

61

"Should we stop in Cambridge for lunch?" Bob asked. We could go to Harvest.

Marcus was driving. "Um, we could, I suppose."

"Come on, let's do it. For old times' sake."

Harvest was a lovely restaurant with very good food, slightly pretentious, like everything in Cambridge. They had been there many times in the days when Marcus taught at Harvard and Bob was in law school.

They hit it at peak lunch hour, and waited for a table at the bar, where Marcus ran into one of his old colleagues, Arthur Banfield.

"Marcus, my God, what are you doing here?"

"Actually we're just passing through on the way to Maine. You remember Bob, my partner."

"Yes of course." They shook hands.

"So how is life in Nirvana?"

"Oh, you know, perfect." It wasn't, but Marcus wasn't going to say so.

"Excellent. I read your last piece. Nicely done."

"Thank you," Marcus said, a note of bemusement in his voice. He had published an article on Thoreau in an obscure journal that his colleagues in San Diego didn't really respect. He was surprised Arthur had read it.

"Well, take care." And Arthur was off.

Typical, Marcus thought. *I'm worth exactly ninety seconds to a senior faculty member.*

He also found it interesting that for Arthur, the content of the piece mattered more than the venue. That was the difference, or one of them, between Harvard and UCSD.

Lunch was excellent, and after finishing they drove past the apartment building where they had first lived together.

"Brings back a lot, doesn't it," Bob said wistfully.

"Good memories," Marcus said.

Then they were on the road again. They pulled into Miller's Cove around 3:00, and, as soon as they got off the freeway, turned off the car's air conditioning and opened the windows. They smelled the ocean.

"It's a different smell," Bob said.

"Yeah, it is. The Pacific has attitude. The Atlantic is . . . tame," Marcus said.

They checked into the Hilltop Inn, where they had stayed several times, and the owner greeted them warmly.

"Ah, the old married couple."

"I beg your pardon," Bob said. "I'm thirty-one."

"Metaphorically old. How long have you two been together now?"

"Ten years," Marcus said.

"My God. A world record."

They laughed. They deposited their bags in their room and took the ten-minute walk down to the shore. In front of the beach were long benches covered by an awning, where Marcus had first said 'I love you' to Bob. Seeing it made both of them think of that moment. They paused, and Bob took Marcus's hand.

They walked through the sand to what everyone called "Section B, for Boys." It was jam-packed with gay men.

"Still a thriving resort, I see," Marcus said.

Back at the entrance to the beach they stopped at the concession stand and then sat under the awning.

"God, I can't remember the last time I ate an ice cream cone," Marcus said.

Bob laughed. "That's because you need to watch your figure, or I'll leave you."

They napped for an hour or so at the inn, and for dinner chose Einstein's, the local deli. That, too, brought back memories: it was a lunch there when Marcus first had the sense that Bob might be flirting with him.

They went to bed early, and that night Bob slept better than he had in months. When he woke up, he understood why couples took second honeymoons.

They spent the rest of the week relaxing at the beach or at the inn's pool. Marcus had brought two books he needed to read for work; he sat under the awning, taking notes, while Bob rented a beach chair in Section B and read some mysteries he'd bought at the local bookstore. He felt the tension leaving his body, a little bit every day. The weather was fine, except for one afternoon when it rained. That day they stayed in their room and made love for hours.

Each night they went to one of the local restaurants, including an Italian place they both remembered and liked, and a few nights, after dinner, they stopped by the Veranda, a local piano bar.

Midweek they phoned Danbury, where Ruth said she was getting stronger; then they called the San Diego kennel, whose owner assured them Oscar was fine.

Too soon, their week was up. They drove down to the Boston airport and flew home.

"I'm glad we did that," Bob said.

Marcus smiled.

62

They got back to San Diego, took a cab home, and immediately went to pick up Oscar. Bob sat in the back seat with him, trying to keep him calm, while Marcus drove. When they got home, Oscar went from room to room, making sure everything was as it should be. Then the three of them went outside and played until they were all exhausted.

They went to bed early, still on East Coast time, and Bob got up at 5:00, fed Oscar, played fetch with him, and headed to the office around 7:00.

There was a memo on his desk from Sarah.

Boss: One important message. From Mrs. Yaeger, asking you to call her "during weekday business hours" at this number.

That was interesting. Really interesting.

Sarah, Anna, and Jason all arrived around 9:00; he had told them all to stay out of the office until he got back, but Sarah had checked the phone for messages every few days, as she usually did.

They all looked rested.

"Wow," Jason said. "You're tan."

"East coast tan," Bob said. "It won't last."

At 10:00, he called the number Mrs. Yaeger had left.

"I'm wondering if you could meet me in Laguna Beach one early afternoon. Without my husband. There are some things I think I should share with you."

"Of course," Bob said. They made arrangements to meet that afternoon.

"And please, come alone."

"Certainly," Bob said.

Bob spent time going over pending cases with Anna and Jason, and then left for Laguna Beach.

Mrs. Yaeger opened the door. She was wearing a beautiful print dress and pearls, which, Bob was sure, were the real thing.

"Please, come in. Can I offer you a drink, or coffee? Iced tea?"

"Actually some water would be great."

"With or without fizz?"

"With, if you have it."

She disappeared into the kitchen and came back with a glass of mineral water.

"So. You're probably wondering why I asked to see you."

"Yes."

"There are some things my husband does not know, and I think would upset him. Some things about Cathy."

Bob waited.

"She admitted to me that she had a drug problem. And that she drank too much."

"I see." Bob was very still.

"When did she tell you this?"

"About six months before she died. I offered to send her to Betty Ford, but she didn't want to do that. Instead, she was in therapy. Which I paid for."

"I see."

"Do you know the name of her therapist?"

"I'm sorry, I don't. I gave Cathy the money, and she paid the therapist. After a while, I think Cathy was paying her herself. She said it was important to her to do this herself."

"Do you know what kind of drugs she was taking?"

"I don't. I only know she said they were easy to get."

She paused, then went on. "There's more. She told me Kenny was very supportive."

"Did she say in what way?"

"No. He just said he really cared about her, and he realized that substances affected her more than they affected him."

Bob was taking notes. He tried to get her words down exactly.

"I didn't tell my husband any of this. He would have been very upset. In many ways, Cathy was still daddy's little girl. I guess that's somewhat to be expected."

Bob waited to see if there was more. When there wasn't, he spoke.

"Thank you, Mrs. Yaeger, for telling me all of this. I'm sure it's painful to talk about."

"Yes, it is." She took a sip of her iced tea.

"I'm afraid I can't keep this confidential. It's evidence, and Kenny is charged with murder."

"I understand. I've spoken to my attorney, and he has said the same thing. He said I will need to testify at Ken's trial."

Bob waited.

Mrs. Yaeger took a deep breath. "I'm willing to do that."

"Thank you. Would you also be willing to give a sworn deposition, just repeating what you've said here, that I can show to the district attorney? That might lead him to drop the charges, which would spare you a courtroom appearance."

"I . . . I don't know." She seemed a bit flustered, for the first time. "I'll need to ask my attorney. I'll let you know."

"I appreciate that. And again, thank you."

"This isn't easy. And I hope . . ."

"Yes."

"I hope it doesn't end my marriage." She smiled a very sad smile.

63

When Bob got back to San Diego, he called Jason and Anna into his inner office and told them what had transpired.

"Holy shit," Jason said.

"I mean, if she does a deposition, won't they have to drop the charges?" Anna asked.

"I don't know. And she may not do a deposition. My guess is she won't—she will want to be subpoenaed, so that she can tell her husband she had no choice but to testify."

"I see," Anna said. "He doesn't know."

"No. She hasn't told him any of this, apparently."

"So we wait," Jason said.

"We wait."

Marcus took care of some paper work and then left the office early, still jet lagged but feeling better about Kenny's case. When he got home Marcus was sitting alone in the living room, no book in his lap, no music playing. Something was wrong.

"What's up?" hoping it wasn't a phone call from Danbury.

"I didn't get my merit. I went to the office, talked to Stanley."

Stanley was Marcus's program chair, and merit reviews at the University of California were performance reviews. As an associate professor, Marcus went through one every two years. They determined salary, and also status.

"But you had that new article," Bob said.

"Not enough, apparently. 'Too few pages' were Stanley's exact words."

"They count pages? That's ridiculous. Can you appeal?"

"I can't appeal as an individual, but the program could. Only Stanley said he took soundings while we were away, and they won't."

"Why not? Come into the kitchen." Bob poured them both a glass of white wine.

"My 'performance,'" Stanley said, "has been 'somewhat disappointing.' My progress has been too slow."

"But you're working on a book."

"Yes, and until it's published, it looks like I'm not working hard."

"What crap."

"I mean, I know I have to perform. We all do. You perform in the courtroom, right? I perform in the classroom, and I'm supposed to perform professionally. But . . ."

"But?"

"I'm a square peg in a very round hole."

"How do you mean?"

"My work doesn't divide up neatly into articles that can be published in peer-reviewed journals. I mean that one piece did, it could stand on its own, but mostly, I write books."

"And a major university can't understand that?"

"Well, this one doesn't. Like I say, square peg, round hole."

Bob didn't know what to say. "Well, you're my square peg." Marcus smiled for the first time.

"I know," Bob said, "take some time off. Finish the book. We can use some of the Kandinsky money."

Marcus shook his head. "I don't want to touch that."

"Why not? We did when I needed it. We should use it. It's been earning interest, I'll bet we wouldn't even need to touch the principal."

"Maybe. I'll think about it. It's too late to take the fall off, but maybe winter and spring." UCSD was on a quarter system.

"Let's drive out to the beach for dinner." Bob thought that would cheer Marcus up.

"No, let's stay in. I'm beat. We can order in."

"Okay. Where's his majesty?"

"Penny took him for a walk." Marcus looked at his watch. "They'll be back soon."

"Take a shower. I'll order dinner. Then we'll go out for ice cream."

"Okay, but if we run into anyone from campus, we're leaving."

64

Over the next few days, Bob did his best to cheer Marcus up. He told him they may have gotten a big break in the case, one that should turn suspicion away from Kenny. Marcus was glad to hear it.

"Has he been in touch with you?" Bob asked. "I mean about his academic work?"

"No. As far as I know, no one on campus has heard from him."

At the office, Jason said he and Kenny had finished their drive-arounds to houses where Kenny and Cathy had done their thing. One or two were in San Diego, a couple in Los Angeles, and one in Palm Springs.

"I've been checking backgrounds. Several are minor Hollywood types, screenwriters, associate producers, an actor, that type of thing."

"That corroborates part of Kenny's story. He said they did these things in part because Cathy wanted Hollywood connections."

"Mostly they're men in their forties or fifties, most of them divorced. And . . ."

"And?"

"We may have hit paydirt. One of them has a record for domestic battery."

"Wow. Details?"

"His name is Peter Arnold. He's an associate producer at MGM. He was married, briefly, to a woman named Audrey Sanders, an actress. Twice, police were called to their house in Santa Monica. Both of those times the charges were dropped.

But there was a third incident where he apparently beat her pretty bad. He was charged and eventually took a plea bargain. Suspended sentence. And he lost a lot in the divorce."

"When was this?"

"About three years ago."

"Did Kenny participate in any of their visits? Or was it just Cathy?"

"He says it was just Cathy. He would drive her to his house in Palm Springs, and then he would go to a restaurant, or whatever."

"Did you believe him?"

Jason shrugged.

"Is Palm Springs a second home for this guy?"

"It was. Now he lives there full time. Since the divorce."

"Okay. Good. Get Sarah to see if she can set up an interview. I want to talk to him."

"And what about the others?" Jason asked.

Bob thought for a moment. "Let's hold off for now."

Bob went back to work on other cases. Late in the day, Sarah reported that she had reached Arnold and that he wanted to talk to Bob before agreeing to meet. She handed him a slip of paper with the phone number.

Bob called, got an answering machine. He left a brief message with his phone numbers, including his home phone.

Arnold called that night as Bob and Marcus were finishing dinner. Bob explained the situation. Arnold was extremely reluctant to meet.

"The thing is Mr. Arnold, you could be subpoenaed. If that happens, you would have to give a recorded deposition, under oath. At this point, if you agree to meet with us, it can be an informal conversation. At least for now."

There was a long pause. "All right. Have your people call

this number, set up a meeting." He gave Bob a phone number. When he got off the phone, he was smiling.

"Another break?" Marcus asked.

"Could be. We'll see."

65

While Sarah tried to reach Peter Arnold's "people" to arrange a meeting, Bob and Anna worked together on a number of other pending cases. Late one afternoon, as they were huddling over Bob's computer, Sarah buzzed to say Mrs. Yaeger was on the line. Bob picked up immediately.

"Mrs. Yaeger."

"Hello Mr. Abramson. I've spoken with my attorney about what you asked. He advises me against sitting for a deposition. I will, however, answer a subpoena and testify at Mr. Glick's trial if it's absolutely necessary."

It was what Bob expected. "I'm afraid it would be, if the case does go to trial. There is some chance that it won't."

"I see. Well, let's hope not. I'm sure you can appreciate how delicate this matter is, for my family."

"Yes, of course. And I'm very grateful that you are willing to testify."

"Can you tell me, how is Kenny handling all of this?"

Bob didn't expect that.

"About as well as can be expected. But a murder charge is extremely serious. Of course."

They discussed the trial date and Bob thanked her for calling.

"No deposition," Anna said when he got off the phone.

"No deposition. In a way, that's good. Her testimony would have a huge impact on the jury. If . . ."

"If?"

"If she sticks to her story. I've seen witnesses change their tune once they get on the stand. It doesn't happen often, but it happens."

Sarah buzzed again. "The interview with Arnold is set for Friday in Palm Springs. 11:00 a.m."

66

To get to Palm Springs, Bob and Jason left San Diego at 7:30. Bleary-eyed, Bob got up at 5:00, took care of Oscar, and dressed carefully.

"Palm Springs." Marcus said. "It will be 110 degrees. In the shade."

"I know. But this is important."

They had visited Palm Springs one winter and found it beautiful but strange. The weather was warm and dry during the day and cold at night, but not too cold. The air was clear. The city sat in a valley surrounded by both close and distant mountains, and during the day you could lounge by the pool and stare off at snowy peaks, which felt unsettling and peaceful at the same time, like most of California, only more so.

The city had a large gay population; houses were affordable since the summers were so hot. Before air conditioning, the city would empty out in the hot months, but now some people lived there year-round. Tourism was the main industry.

Socially it was an odd mix. Retired couples and singles,

gay and straight, and rich folks with second homes they visited only in winter. The gay community there seemed built to deliver sex on demand, with several clothing-optional resorts and lots of bars. The straight community seemed to be organized around several lavish country clubs. Pools and golf courses were everywhere.

When Bob and Jason visited their witness, it was mid-July, blazing hot, and the sun was blinding. It was dry heat, but, as Marcus had said once when he went to a conference in Phoenix in early June, above 90 degrees, hot was hot.

Getting out of the car was like walking into an oven. Arnold's house was stucco painted white, with a brick driveway and a dark blue BMW parked in front. There were a few narrow windows facing the front.

They rang the bell, and a handsome, fiftyish man opened the door.

"Come in. I'm Peter Arnold." He was dressed in a very expensive-looking white linen suit, a blue shirt open at the collar, and loafers with no socks; he reminded Bob of the prep school boys he'd known, but not liked, at Brown and in law school.

The house, icy cool inside, was built around a courtyard with a lap pool and large windows and glass doors everywhere. Arnold showed them into a living room: hardwood floors, expensive-looking gray leather furniture, a huge television screen. A fireplace surrounded in blue tile. A tray holding a carafe of coffee and a pitcher of iced tea was waiting.

"Can I offer you a drink?"

"Thanks, yes." Bob accepted coffee and Jason took a glass of iced tea, as did Arnold.

They arranged themselves on two couches facing each other. Bob noticed a pile of what looked like scripts on the coffee table in between.

"So," Arnold said, "you're defending Glick."

"Yes." Bob paused, then said, "Can you tell us what was the nature of your relationship with Catherine Yaeger?"

"It was a personal relationship."

"Was it intimate?"

Arnold sipped. "Yes."

"How often did you meet?"

Arnold considered. "Five times. Maybe six or seven."

"Here is Palm Springs?"

"Yes."

"How did you meet?"

"We met at a party at her parents' beach house, in Laguna Beach."

"When?"

"About fifteen months ago."

"How were you acquainted with Mr. and Mrs. Yaeger?"

"Yaeger is an investor in some of my film projects."

"And how did things proceed after you met?"

"She had given me her phone number at the end of the party. She was flirty." He paused and smiled. "As I remember, it was an afternoon party on a Sunday. Lots of people there. She told me she was an actress. I called her."

"Was Mr. Glick at this party?"

"No. At least, not that I know of."

"So you invited her here?"

"Yes."

"And?"

"Her intentions were obvious. I mean, she was dressed like Sharon Stone in *Basic Instinct*. Except she looked more like Liz Taylor, before Liz got so plump. Same coloring as Liz."

"And?"

"And we had sex and then talked about Hollywood."

"I know this is very personal, but how would you describe your sexual relationship?"

"Well," Arnold took a long sip of his tea, looking for the right word, "it was intense."

"By which you mean what, exactly? I'm sorry, but I have to ask."

"Well, Cathy liked to pretend to be in charge. She would call me her sex slave. It was all a performance, but a good one. I got the sense . . ."

"Yes?"

"I think she was trying to show me she could act."

"And you had no objections to that?"

"No. It was a nice change of pace. She was good at it."

"Did Mr. Glick ever participate?"

"No. I never really met him, except to nod to him when he would pick Cathy up."

"Did you ever offer Ms. Yaeger money?"

He paused, sipped his drink. "Once she asked to 'borrow' $400. I knew I wouldn't get it back. I gave it to her."

"Did you ever visit Ms. Yaeger in San Diego?"

"Yes, a couple of times."

Bob and Jason exchanged a quick glance, trying not to show any reaction.

"How did that happen?"

"I go down there sometimes to see people. Friends, business associates. I called her."

"Did you meet at her apartment?"

"Yes."

"Did you have sex there?"

"Yes."

"So it wasn't always here in Palm Springs."

"No."

"When was the last time you were in San Diego?"

"Let me get my calendar." He got up, went to another room, and came back.

"Last week of February. I remember now. A friend there had invited me to a party."

"Did you take Ms. Yaeger to that party?"

"I invited her, but she said she didn't have anything to wear."

"So you saw her after?"

"Yes."

"Did you stay overnight?"

"No."

"Did you ever do drugs with Ms. Yaeger? Or offer them to her?"

"I'd prefer not to answer that."

"All right. For the record, where were you on May eighteenth and nineteenth?"

He looked again in his calendar. "Here. My part-time secretary was here both days, and the night of the eighteenth, I had a dinner party."

"We'll need those names, just to be thorough."

"No problem." He got a pad and pen and started writing. Then he handed the list to Bob, who handed it to Jason.

"Thank you for your time, Mr. Arnold. Assuming Mr. Glick's trial goes forward, I'm afraid we will have to subpoena you to testify."

"I expected that. It won't be the first time." He let out a laugh.

They all stood and walked to the front door.

"Your sidekick here," Arnold said as he walked them to the door, sizing up Jason.

"Yes?" Jason said.

"You could have a future in films, you know. You look like Tab Hunter. That look is getting popular again."

Jason suppressed a smile. "Thanks, but not for me."

"Ah, well."

And with that, Jason and Bob walked back into the oven. They got into Bob's car as quickly as possible and turned the air conditioning up to high.

"You didn't ask him about his record," Jason said.

"No. I'll spring that on him at the trial. I'll ask him about seeing Cathy in San Diego and then bring up his record. Let the jury draw the inference."

"He may not have killed her. I mean, why would he?"

"He may not have done it, sure. But all it takes is a juror or two to think he might have. And to see that the police overlooked him."

"So that's why you didn't ask him if the police had contacted him."

"Right."

"Clever."

"And that's why . . ."

". . . they pay you the big bucks," Jason finished for him.

Arnold's persona made Bob feel like he had just made a soft porn movie. He was glad to get out of Palm Springs . . . but he was glad he had gone.

They were quiet for a while. Finally, Jason spoke.

"Interesting, isn't it, that everyone so far has an alibi? I mean, the people we've been able to find who might be suspects."

"Yeah. It is."

67

A few nights later, Marcus and Bob had their friends Miles and Steve over for dinner. Bob baked pastitsio using freshly ground lamb and noodles from a Greek-owned deli. They served it cold on the patio, Oscar under the table, as ever, pretending to sleep but really on the alert for dropped food. Bob had baked a cherry cobbler for dessert—his mother's recipe.

"So, we wanted to talk to you about something serious," Marcus said.

"Oh? Not too serious, I hope, I've had too much wine," Miles said, laughing.

"No, nothing awful. But we're thinking of adopting," Bob said as he poured them all more decaf.

"Oh, that's wonderful!" Steve said.

Miles and Steve had adopted a baby girl from China. She was now five.

"How did you arrange things?" Bob asked.

"We did it through a lawyer in Los Angeles. We can give you her name. There's a screening process, of course, home visits, paperwork, and a then lot of waiting. But it was worth it," Steve said.

"It was. Absolutely. Best thing we've done," Miles said, putting his hand on top of Steve's.

"It's a big adjustment, of course," Steve said. "And a steep learning curve. But you get the hang of it pretty quickly."

"Any regrets?"

"No, none," Miles said. Steve nodded.

"How do you manage childcare when you're both gone?" Bob asked.

"We hired a nanny. Full time. It's not cheap, but if you hire someone fulltime, you get to know them, and trust them. Maya is in school now during the day, so we don't need her as often," Miles said.

"Do it," Steve said. "You won't regret it."

Bob and Marcus smiled at each other and soon the conversation turn to other things.

After their friends left, Bob said, "so what do you think?"

Marcus looked pensive as he cleared the table. "It's a huge thing. And we'd probably need a bigger house."

"That's true," Bob said, "I hadn't thought of that."

"But they were convincing. I mean, their faces lit up."

Bob felt hopeful.

"Let's mull," Marcus said.

Bob nodded, content to leave it at that, but he did call Miles a few days later and got the name of the attorney in LA.

68

For the next few months, Marcus worked hard on his book; he was very glad his classes didn't start until late September. He had slowly agreed that Bob was right about taking time off, and he informed his program he would be gone for the winter and spring quarters. They weren't happy, and Marcus didn't care, which Bob thought was a good sign.

Meanwhile, Bob had various cases to deal with, mostly DUIs and drug charges, a few domestic disputes. There were no new developments in the Glick case. One night Marcus told Bob that Kenny was taking a leave of absence from his graduate program.

"Not really a surprise," Marcus said. "Still, upsetting. He really is a very good student. Or was."

In October, as the weather turned just a bit cooler, Bob began preparing for Kenny's trial. He met with the judge and Billy Lewis for a pre-trial conference, and, much to his surprise, there were no new depositions from prosecution witnesses.

"I want a clean trial here," Judge Murphy told them, looking from one to the other. "No funny stuff. I mean it. This is a murder trial. No tricks, no grandstanding."

The two lawyers nodded.

A week later Bob and Billy exchanged their lists of witnesses. The prosecution's list was short: The pathologist who performed the autopsy for the family. Maureen Freeman, Jane Masters, Susan Tierney.

"This is pitiful," Bob said to Anna and Jason. "They must have more, or they wouldn't be going to trial."

"And," Anna said, "if they spring a surprise, what happens?"

"We object. Strenuously. Which might or might not work. I've seen it go both ways."

The defense list included Robert Goldstein and Melinda Ivanov, the lead detective on the case, Peter Arnold, Andy Rich from Diversionary, and Cathy's mother.

When Billy got Bob's list, he called.

"Do you have depositions from Arnold and Mrs. Yaeger?" he asked Bob.

"No."

"Why not?" He tried to sound stern, but it was clear to Bob he was just going through the motions.

"Mrs. Yaeger is . . . a reluctant witness. She was advised by her attorney not to be deposed in advance of the trial. She'll require a subpoena to testify. I didn't depose Arnold because I expected you to drop the charges. You know your case is virtually non-existent."

"In your dreams, counselor," was Billy's reply. But Bob knew him well enough to know it was said without conviction.

As he usually did for important trials, Bob began practice sessions, with Anna and Jason playing the part of various witnesses.

"This is fun," Anna said. "I've never done this before."

At the same time, Bob drafted his opening statement to the jury. He debated hiring a jury consultant, but decided it wasn't really necessary in this case because the prosecution had so little to go on. Besides, he told himself, consultants were expensive, and often their suggestions were common sense.

Things were going well, and then, one afternoon, Sarah buzzed him to say his brother was on the line.

"Bobby, it's Mom," Alex said. Bob knew it was bad news. Alex hadn't called him Bobby since seventh grade.

69

"She's been doing really well," Alex said. "We were there a couple of weeks ago. With Jay. She really seemed to be like her old self."

"I know, I've spoken to her a couple of times."

"She had a seizure."

"A seizure?"

"A fainting spell. And then she blacked out."

Bob closed his eyes.

"And?"

"They did scans. The cancer has spread to her brain."

Bob was speechless.

"Bob, are you there?"

"What happens now?"

"Dad insisted on taking her to Sloan Kettering in New York. They're doing tests there, but they're saying they will almost certainly need to operate."

"When?"

"Unclear. Meanwhile she's on some anti-seizure meds that really knock her out. She mostly sleeps. Dad's a basket case."

"Okay. We work out a schedule so that one of us is there at all times."

"Don't you have a murder trial coming up?"

"Jesus, yes. I'll ask for a postponement. What about you?"

"Nothing like that. The usual. And of course I'm in a firm. There are others I can hand things off to when I need to."

"How is Dad?"

"He sounds like a zombie. Carol is flying out tomorrow."

"Okay. Let's talk tomorrow. Let me call Dad."

"Be prepared. This could be . . ."

Bob cut him off. "Don't say it."

70

Bob dialed the court and spoke to Judge Murphy's clerk. He requested a conference first thing in the morning, and the clerk agreed, assuming Billy Lewis was available. Then he called Billy and told him what was happening.

"Oh, God, Bob, I'm sorry. Of course we'll agree to a postponement."

He gathered up his things are told Sarah he had to leave for the day. He didn't want to tell anyone in the office; that would make it too real.

At home he found their neighbor, Penny, playing fetch with Oscar in the yard.

"You're home early," Penny said.

"Yeah. Headache."

"Do you want me to stay? I can."

"No, that's fine. I'll take over."

As soon as she had gone, Bob poured himself a whiskey and dialed Danbury.

"Dad."

"I know, Bobby. I know."

"What are the doctors saying?"

"They think they can operate without causing any deficits."

"Deficits?"

"That's what they call them. Lasting effects."

"Such as?"

"Let's not talk about that over the phone."

"Okay. I'll fly out as soon as I can."

"What about your murder?"

"I'll ask for a postponement. The prosecutor has already agreed."

"Okay. Carol is coming tomorrow."

"I know. Alex told me. We'll work out a schedule. Like before."

"Okay. I love you, son." And with that, his father hung up.

His father's tone of voice and abruptness terrified Bob almost as much as the news. He drank his scotch. Oscar sat in front of him, looking up; Bob scratched behind his ears.

Then he went into the bedroom and promptly fell asleep.

Marcus came home around 6:00 and Bob stirred.

"What's wrong?"

"Mom."

71

In the morning, Judge Murphy was understanding. "But," she said, "the problem is the calendar. I'm off the second half of December, a family wedding in Ireland. Then I have some major litigation already scheduled for January. It's been postponed twice already, it has to come to trial. So we'd be looking at early February. Your client might not want to wait that long."

"I'll speak to him. If he's willing, Billy, would February be all right with your office?"

"I'll have to check but I don't think there'll be a problem."

"Good," the judge said. "Both of you let me know. For now, let's say, tentatively, Monday February 6th."

Both Bob and Billy nodded.

Billy called Bob's office an hour later to say the date was fine. Bob asked Sarah to get Kenny in for a conference.

He came in at 1:00 and Bob told him the situation.

"If you don't want to wait, I can find you another attorney."

He thought for a moment. "No. Let's just wait. I hope your mom will be okay."

"Thank you. In the meantime, continue to lie low. What are you doing with yourself? Marcus said you took a leave from your program."

"Well, yeah. I mean . . . you know. So I read, I go to the gym. Watch TV. I'm thinking . . ."

"Yes?"

"I'm thinking of going to law school instead of a PhD. That is, if I'm not in jail."

"You won't be in jail. Leave that to me."

After he left, Bob called Sarah, Anna, and Jason into the office and gave them the news.

"We have that DUI trial this week. After that, we'll stop taking new cases. I think everything else can stay on hold. Anna, go through all the pending cases. If there's anything that looks like it's urgent or semi-urgent, we'll find alternate counsel."

"Of course."

Sarah asked if Bob wanted her to make a flight reservation for next week.

"Better hold off. I'll let you know."

After they left him alone, Bob opened the file on the DUI. He didn't think it would take more than a day or, at most, two days in court. He put himself on automatic pilot, as he often did when upset or frightened, and got through the trial. He somehow managed to get his client a suspended sentence, with community service and a fine. Anna, who accompanied him to court, was a big help, slipping him notes as he questioned witnesses.

Later, much later, Bob had only a hazy memory of the following few days. He remembered sleeping a lot. He remembered that on a Saturday, a picture perfect day, Alex called to say brain surgery had been set for the following week.

He remembered calling Sarah at home, who made him a plane reservation and nearly cried, even though she had never met Ruth. He remembered checking into a Manhattan hotel, the same one Alex and Carol were staying at, but he couldn't remember its name. He vaguely remembered his father was staying at a building where Sloan Kettering had studio apartments for the families of patients undergoing surgeries or serious treatments. He remembered a dinner out with his father when both of them said hardly a word.

They had already admitted Ruth to the hospital when he

arrived. She did her best to sound cheerful, but, for the first time in his life, it sounded fake to Bob.

A performance.

He remembered that Marcus canceled his classes and went up to LA to stay with Jay, taking him to school, picking him up, doing his best to cook. He brought Oscar, and he remembered Carol saying Jay was in heaven with two dogs to play with.

The day of the surgery, he remembered going to the hospital really early, with Alex and Carol and his father.

He remembered two surgeons coming to find them after the surgery, with their surgical masks hanging around their necks. They said it went well, they had removed the tumor and that, in time, Ruth would be fine.

"But this will be a long recovery. She may not seem like her old self for a while."

Mostly, he remembered that after the surgeons left, his father started to cry.

72

Carol flew home a day or two later to relieve Marcus. They took Ruth home a week after her surgery, her head still wrapped in bandages. She spoke slowly but could move and talk and see and smell. And even smile.

For the next few weeks, Alex and Carol and Bob took turns flying back and forth across the continent. It was all a blur of tickets and airports and bad airplane food. Jake hired home aides until the bandages came off. Ruth slowly regained her strength. Once a week, Jake drove her into Manhattan for scans, which were consistently clear.

Then it was Thanksgiving, and Carol and Marcus and Jay flew east together and everyone helped prepare a feast. Alex was already there. By then Ruth was beginning to seem like her old self. She sat in the kitchen while everyone was cooking, with Jay next to her; they played gin rummy and Ruth let Jay win every hand.

"You're just too good for me," Ruth said, and Jay laughed and even pranced around the kitchen table.

On Sunday Carol and Jay flew back to LA and Marcus to San Diego. Alex left two days later, and Ruth told Bob to go home a few days later.

"I'm fine. Really. The doctors are happy. I'm getting stronger. Go back to your life. Don't let Marcus live alone for too long, he'll starve to death."

At that, Bob couldn't stop laughing.

He did go home and slowly resumed work. They had all agreed they would assemble again between Christmas and New Year's, when both Jay and Marcus would be free from school.

By then Ruth was looking and sounding more like herself. They cooked, they ate, they played cards and board games with Jay, and took him to see movies, *The Lion King* and *The Flintstones*. It snowed, and Jay loved playing outside in it.

"Why don't we have snow at home?" he asked Alex.

"Because in California we're civilized. We visit the snow in the mountains. Then we go home and swim in the ocean."

Ruth thought that was the funniest thing she ever heard.

They exchanged presents all around one evening in front of the fire, books and sweaters, ties for the men, scarves for the women, and a sled for Jay, for when he visited, Ruth said. He loved it.

And then, on New Year's Eve, after Jay had gone to bed,

Carol said they had an announcement. She took Alex's hand.

"I'm pregnant. It's a girl."

Everyone started to cry.

73

By mid-January Bob was back at work and began trial preparation in earnest. He polished his opening statement, struggling over nearly every word. He knew to keep it short. He typed out his list of questions for each witness, with Anna's input. Marcus worked diligently on his book on the political rhetoric of the 1930s, sometimes at home, sometimes in his office on campus. The nights turned crisp and very cool, as they often did in December and January. They talked more about adopting a baby. Bob was ready to do it, and he could see Marcus getting there.

Finally Kenny's trial date arrived and jury selection began. Anna often had perceptive comments to make about potential jurors, sometimes echoing thoughts Bob had had, sometimes about things that hadn't occurred to him.

"Not him," she whispered about one juror. "He's religious. Or at least moralistic. Look at his expression: very judgmental, don't you think?" They wanted to stay away from religious folks who would be appalled by Kenny's and Carol's sexual behavior, and from non-college-educated jurors, who might resent Kenny's privilege.

In the end a panel of seven women and five men, plus two alternates, was seated, and as Judge Murphy gave them the usual instructions, Bob looked around the courtroom. In the gallery he noticed two local reporters, Kenny's parents, and Cathy's mother. Mr. Yeager was not with her.

The prosecution's opening statement was dramatic. "You will hear," Billy solemnly intoned, "that Mr. Glick and the deceased lived a wild life. There was drinking. There were wild sexual escapades. And there was violence."

He continued for some time, painting a picture of a depraved couple who, clearly, had no moral standards—and, by implication, a young man with no moral limits on what he might do. The contrast between the incorrgible murderer and the handscome, rather naive-looking boy at the defense table could not have been greater.

Bob's statement was succinct.

"Mr. Glick and Ms. Yaeger were not angels. They may well have done things you consider abhorrent. They may have skirted the boundaries of the law. But that does not mean Mr. Glick is guilty of murder. The state must prove Mr. Glick's guilt beyond a reasonable doubt. *Beyond a reasonable doubt.* Keep repeating that phrase in your minds as you listen to the testimony. Mr. Glick may be guilty of several things, but murder is not one of them."

Bob had told Kenny not to be afraid to look at the jury, and he wasn't. "Do your best to look angelic," Bob told him. "And do not fidget. Stay still and calm."

The prosecution's first witness was the pathologist the Yaeger family had hired to do the second autopsy, a very young doctor named Willoughby. He testified that in his opinion Catherine Yaeger died from strangulation during a rape. The photos from the second autopsy were shown on a large screen at the front of the courtroom, causing a stir among the jurors and the spectators. The judge banged her gavel and demanded quiet.

On cross-examination, Bob pushed him hard.

"Is it possible, Dr. Willoughby, that the injuries you observed were inflicted a day or two or even three before Ms. Yaeger's death?"

"I don't think they were."

"But is it not the case that such marks as these"—Bob pointed to the screen to show the jury that he was not afraid of the images—"can take up to seventy-two hours to develop?"

"I don't think . . ."

Bob cut him off. "Is it possible, doctor? That is a yes-or-no question."

There was a long pause. "It's possible."

"So then it is also possible that Ms. Yaeger died from other causes, is it not? Yes or no, doctor."

"It is possible."

"Thank you."

"Redirect, Mr. Lewis?"

"No further questions, Your Honor."

The next witnesses were the two undergraduates, and Bob had a relatively easy time challenging their credibility. Jane Masters and Maureen Freeman were completely vague about what she had seen and heard, and where, and when.

"Ms. Freeman, do you recall meeting with me?"

"Yes."

"When we met, do you recall telling me you did not know Mr. Glick and had never really spoken to him?"

"Yes."

"Your Honor, I ask that this be marked Defense Exhibit One." He held two sheets of computer paper, which he showed to the judge and then to Billy Lewis.

"So ordered."

Bob gave the pages to Maureen.

"Ms. Freeman, what is printed on these pages?"

She swallowed hard.

"Ms. Freeman?"

"It looks like a class list."

"Would you look at the name checked off with a red mark. Whose name is that?"

She shot Bob a hateful look. "Mine."

"Is it not true, Ms. Freeman, that you were enrolled as a student in a section of the course 'Introduction to American Government' taught by the defendant in the winter quarter of 1993?"

"Yes."

"So you did know Mr. Glick, did you not?"

"Yes. But . . ."

Bob cut her off. "That will be all, thank you Ms. Freeman."

"You may step down," Judge Murphy said. "And young lady, I suggest when you get back to campus, you go to the library and look up the meaning of the word 'perjury.'"

That was icing on the cake for Bob. He tried not to smile. Billy Lewis shut his eyes.

"Court will be in recess until nine a.m. tomorrow." Murphy banged her gavel.

In the hallway, Bob told Kenny, not for the first time, that he needed to know his secret weapon against Susan Tierney.

"She'll be on the stand tomorrow. Now's the time, Kenny. In fact it's long past time. I probably should have interviewed her sooner."

"Don't cross-examine her. Recall her when we present our defense."

"Kenny," Bob said, getting irritated, "did you go to law school when I wasn't looking?"

"Abramson, trust me. I know what I'm doing." And with

that, he joined his parents, who were standing at a respectful distance. They nodded to Bob.

Bob wondered what the hell was going on. "Abramson"?

74

The next day, Lewis first called Rebecca Morrison to the stand. She testified that she had heard and seen Kenny and Cathy arguing "several times."

"Did you think these were just normal arguments, the kind that couples often have?"

Bob objected to the question. "The witness is not a psychologist or a psychiatrist. She is not qualified to answer that question."

The judge overruled the objection. "The witness may answer."

"Well, no. I thought they were not typical."

She then added that she "thought" she'd heard a "terrible" argument between them the night before Cathy was found dead.

On cross-examination, Bob read various lines from Ms. Morrison's deposition. She confirmed that on the night in question, she had been lying down without her hearing aid, and that she had not put it back in when she heard the argument.

"So, Ms. Morrison, you don't know for sure who was arguing that night."

"Well, I . . ."

"Yes?"

"No. I'm not sure."

"Thank you."

Lewis jumped to his feet. "Redirect, Your Honor?"

Murphy nodded.

"Ms. Morrison, was what you heard that evening consistent with the kinds of arguments you had heard between these two young people on previous occasions, when you were wearing your hearing aid?"

"Consistent?"

"Yes, consistent. Did what you heard that night match what you had heard before?"

"Well, I . . ." She looked over at Bob and Kenny.

"Please answer, Ms. Morrison," the judge said.

"I don't know for sure."

Lewis dismissed the witness and returned to his chair, clearly unhappy.

The next witness was Susan Tierney. For the first time, Bob felt nervous.

"Ms. Tierney, you shared an apartment with Catherine Yaeger, is that correct?"

"Yes."

"So you had a chance to observe Ms. Yaeger and the defendant together?"

"Yes."

"How often?"

"Quite often. We sometimes had dinner together, and Kenny stayed over quite a bit. Two or three times a week."

"Did Ms. Yaeger talk to you about Mr. Glick?"

"Yes."

"And what did she say?"

Bob objected. "That is hearsay, Your Honor. This testimony should not be allowed."

"Ms. Yaeger is dead," Billy responded. "And given the closeness of her relationship to this witness, this clearly qualifies as an exception to the rules governing hearsay."

"I agree. Overruled. The witness may answer."

"She said that she was afraid of Kenny, and that she wanted to end the relationship."

There was murmuring in the courtroom, and Judge Murphy banged her gavel.

"Did she say this on more than one occasion?"

"Yes. Several times."

"Did you ask her why she didn't end the relationship?"

"Yes. Once."

"And what did she say?"

"She said Ken was helping her earn money, and that she needed the money."

More murmuring. Another bang of the gavel.

"Did she say how he was helping her earn money?"

"No."

Billy walked back to his table. "Your witness."

"No questions at this time, Your Honor," Bob said, "but we reserve the right to recall this witness to the stand at a later time."

"You may step down, Miss."

"Mr. Lewis?"

"The State calls James Cunningham."

Bob leapt to his feet and objected.

"Your Honor, this witness was not on the prosecution's list."

"Counsel approach."

At the bench, Murphy asked Billy why Cunningham's name was not on his witness list.

"Your Honor, we only received word in the last twenty-four hours that this witness had relevant information and was willing to testify."

Murphy paused for a moment. "If I find that is not the case, Mr. Lewis, I will strike his testimony and might well declare a mistrial. Now step back."

Bob went back to his seat, and Billy approached the witness.

"Mr. Cunningham, were you acquainted with Catherine Yaeger and Kenneth Glick?"

"Yes."

"And what was the nature of your relationship?"

"It was sexual."

"With both of them at the same time?"

"At times. At times with one, alone, and at times with the other, alone."

Shocked noises arose from the courtroom.

The judge banged her gavel several times. "If there are any more outbursts, I will clear the courtroom."

"Mr. Cunningham, did you give money to Ms. Yaeger and Mr. Glick?"

"Yes."

"Each time?"

"Yes."

"No further questions."

Bob rose.

"Mr. Cunningham, did Ms. Yaeger or Mr. Glick ask you for money before your intimate encounters."

"No."

"So you gave them money after having sex?"

"Yes."

"Why?"

Cunningham smiled. "Because I was pleased with their performance."

"Did they at any time request or demand money?"

"No."

"So you gave it to them of your own free will?"

"Yes, I did."

"So it was a gift, would you say?"

"Yes. That's exactly what it was."

"Have you given money to other individuals with whom you have had sexual relations?"

"Yes. If not money, presents."

"What is your net worth, Mr. Cunningham?"

He seemed surprised by the question.

"I can only give you an approximate figure."

"And what would that figure be?"

"Roughly $250 million."

Low murmurs in the courtroom.

"No further questions."

"Mr. Lewis?"

"The state rests, Your Honor."

"We will reconvene tomorrow at 10 a.m." Judge Murphy banged her gavel and quickly left.

Kenny started to say something to Bob, who whispered "not here." They walked out of the courtroom into the hallway.

"Do you have any idea, Kenny, how the prosecution found Cunningham?"

"No. I don't."

"Are you sure?"

"Yes!"

"Have you been in touch with him?"

Kenny looked down. "Yes."

Bob tried to control his temper. "Tell me."

"About a week ago he called, invited me to lunch. I've been going stir crazy, so I accepted."

"Where did you meet for lunch?"

"At a restaurant in La Jolla."

"And you didn't think to tell me?"

Kenny didn't answer.

"Do you realize you were probably followed? By the police."

"I'm sorry."

"Sorry doesn't cut it, Kenny." He was getting really angry. Anna put her hand on Bob's arm. He calmed down.

"I want what you have on Susan Tierney. Now. Meet me back at my office."

75

Bob drove to his office, undid his tie, and took a bottle of scotch out of the bottom drawer of his desk. He offered some to Anna, who shook her head. He took a swig directly from the bottle.

Fifteen minutes later, Kenny showed up with someone Bob had never seen before. Kenny introduced him as Alan Clark. He was about Kenny's age and looked like a typical native Californian, blond, tan, fit, a younger version of Jason.

Bob shook his hand.

"Alan, tell Mr. Abramson what you know about Susan Tierney."

76

Anna offered to drive Bob home after Kenny and Alan Clark had left. He looked quietly furious.

He calmed down, then said, "No, I'm fine. I'll drive myself."

Marcus was cooking his reliable tuna casserole. Bob

poured himself another scotch. A double.

"That bad?"

"Oh, yeah. When will that be ready? I want to take a bath."

"It'll keep."

When Bob came back to the kitchen, Marcus asked him what was up.

"I don't want to talk about it, I'll get too angry. But it will probably be on the front page of tomorrow's paper." He let out a little laugh.

When the phone rang, he said, "Don't answer, it will be a reporter."

Marcus answered. It was a reporter. "I'm sorry, he's not available."

"Take it off the hook."

They went to bed early and got up early.

The morning paper had its three-column article about James Cunningham's testimony on the front page.

"Jesus. I had no idea. Did you?"

"Yes."

"And you didn't tell me??"

"Client confidentiality. Even Kenneth Glick is entitled to that."

"Do you think he's guilty? Of the murder, I mean." Marcus had avoided asking that question for months.

"No, I don't. But he's not my favorite human being."

They ate breakfast in silence. Bob wished he could have told Marcus more about Kenny, though they both knew he was restrained by privilege. Sensing his frustration, Marcus regretted involving Bob in such a complicated, and unpleasant, case. But neither of them spoke.

After breakfast Bob called the judge's clerk. He left a message. "Please make sure Susan Tierney is in the court when we reconvene. She will be my first witness."

Bob left for his office to make some notes before heading to court. Anna came in and they talked strategy. He told her in what order he intended to call witnesses, and tasked her to make sure they were available.

77

Court was called into session at exactly 10:00 a.m., with the usual "All Rise" from the clerk. Judge Murphy took her chair and told everyone to sit.

"Mr. Abramson?"

"The defense recalls Susan Tierney."

Susan walked slowly to the stand. She was wearing a white blouse and a dark blue skirt, and high heels.

"You are still under oath, Ms. Tierney," the judge said, and she nodded.

Bob walked over to the jury box and rested his arms on the railing, looking at the jurors. He paused for a long moment before approaching the witness stand.

"Ms. Tierney, were you attracted to Mr. Glick?" Bob turned slowly toward her.

She looked indignant. "No, I was not."

"So at no time did you hope to have a relationship with Mr. Glick?"

"No. Never."

Bob walked back to his table and paused again. He looked at some notes, and then looked up.

"Ms. Tierney, how many times have you been admitted to the Psychiatric Hospital at UCLA?"

Rustling and whispering erupted in the courtroom. Judge Murphy banged her gavel twice.

"Ms. Tierney? How many times?"

She looked down.

"Four."

"When were you last there?"

"About three months ago."

More murmuring. Another bang of the gavel.

"I know this is difficult to talk about. But what condition or conditions were being treated at the hospital?"

She looked down. "Manic-depression and schizophrenia."

Again murmuring followed by the gavel.

"Isn't it true that you once spent nearly an entire year confined there?"

"Yes," she said quietly.

"In between hospital stays, did you consult a psychiatrist?"

"Yes." Once again, a flash of indignation crossed Susan's face.

"And are you currently taking medications for these conditions?"

"Yes."

"Have you consistently taken your medications over the last several years?"

She looked down again. "At times I've stopped. They have side effects."

Bob could see that the testimony was having the desired effect on the judge, and the jury.

"No further questions."

"Mr. Lewis?"

Billy looked completely flummoxed. "I have no questions, Your Honor."

Susan Tierney did her best to compose herself as she left

the stand. She did not look at Bob or at Kenny.

"The defense calls Alan Clark."

Billy quickly looked through papers on his table and then jumped up. "Your Honor, this witness was not mentioned in discovery."

"Counsel approach."

Before the judge's bench, Bob explained that the witness had just been brought to his attention. The judge agreed to allow the testimony, pending a possible ruling on relevance, and sent them back to their seats. Bob stood in front of his table as Clark was sworn in.

"Mr. Clark, do you know Susan Tierney?"

"Yes. We've known each other since eighth grade. We grew up near each other in Encino."

"Did you ever have a romantic relationship?"

"Briefly, yes. About eight months ago."

"And during that relationship, did Ms. Tierney mention the defendant, Kenneth Glick?"

"Yes. Constantly. She was obsessed with him."

Murmuring, gavel.

"What do you mean?"

"She talked about him all the time. How attractive he was. How much she wanted to be with him. And there were times . . ."

He hesitated.

"Please go on."

"We only were intimate a few times. But when we were, she would call me Kenny. During sex."

Loud murmuring, and furious gaveling by the judge.

"Did you ever point that out to her?"

"Yes."

"And how did she respond?"

"She said I was a stand-in, and laughed."

"Thank you. No further questions."

Judge Murphy turned toward Billy, her eyebrows arced.

"No questions."

"The witness is excused."

78

After a recess, the trial resumed, and Bob called Christina Yaeger to the stand.

Cathy's mother rose and walked to the stand. She was wearing an expensive-looking white suit with a gray blouse and pearls.

"Your Honor, I'd like the record to reflect that Mrs. Yaeger is here under subpoena."

"So ordered."

"Mrs. Yaeger. Did your daughter Catherine ever talk to you about her personal problems?"

Billy Lewis rose to object to the testimony.

"Save it, Mr. Lewis. You know this falls under the hearsay exception, the same one you used."

Billy sat back down.

"Mrs. Yaeger?"

"Yes, she did."

"What were those personal problems?"

"Cathy had a substance abuse problem. Addictions."

"To what substances?"

"Alcohol and drugs."

Murmurs in the courtroom. Murphy banged her gavel.

"Were they serious addictions?"

"Yes. I offered to send her to the Betty Ford Clinic, but she wanted to stay in San Diego. She started seeing a therapist."

"Did your daughter also talk to you about her relationship with Kenneth Glick?"

"Yes."

"And what did she say?"

"She said that Ken was aware of her problems and trying to help her. She said that he realized that drinking and drugs affected her differently than they affected him."

Bob paused, letting that sink in.

"Did Catherine ever tell you she was afraid of Mr. Glick?"

"No. Quite the opposite. I think she cared about him. She said he cared about her. She thought the relationship might last."

"Was your husband aware of any of this?"

"No." She looked down at her well-manicured hands.

"Thank you, Mrs. Yaeger."

Billy had no questions.

Bob walked back to the defense table. Anna had scribbled a note: "Jury riveted."

The judge said the court would be in recess for twenty minutes; a mid-morning bathroom break, Bob knew. When they returned, he called Dr. Robert Goldstein to the stand.

"Doctor Goldstein, you performed the state's autopsy on Catherine Yaeger, did you not?"

"Yes."

"And what did you find?"

"I found large quantities of alcohol and Demerol in her system. Demerol is a powerful opiate medication."

"Was that the cause of death?"

"Yes. The combination of drugs, given the deceased small stature, stopped her heart."

"Were there any bruises on Ms. Yaeger's neck or around her vagina?"

"No. None."

"You've seen the photos from the second autopsy."

"Yes."

"How do you explain the appearance of those bruises?"

"In my medical opinion, those minor bruises were inflicted twenty-four to seventy-two hours before the death. Such bruises often take that long to appear."

"And you consider those bruises to be minor?"

"Yes."

"No further questions."

"Mr. Lewis?" the judge asked.

Billy rose. He asked if it was possible for strangulation to have been the cause of death.

"No, not in my medical opinion."

"Why not?"

"Neck bruises would have to have been severe, and they would have started to appear by the time of the autopsy. And there would have been changes in the deceased's lungs to indicate death by strangulation."

"Is it possible that cutting off some of Catherine Yaeger's air during sexual intercourse contributed to her death?"

"I don't—"

Billy cut him off. "Yes or no, please, doctor."

"It's a remote possibility, yes. Very remote."

"Nothing further."

Bob rose. "Redirect, Your Honor?" Murphy nodded.

"Dr. Goldstein, would cutting off some of Catherine Yaeger's air during sex have caused her death in the absence of the drugs and alcohol in her body?"

"No."

"No?"

Billy jumped to his feet. "Asked and answered, Your Honor."

Judge Murphy looked sternly at Billy, then at Goldstein. "The witness may elaborate."

"It's true that some individuals find minor choking to be sexually stimulating. But such activity, if it caused or even contributed to her death, would almost certainly have left some evidence in her vocal cords or lungs, or on the neck. There was no such evidence."

"No further questions."

Goldstein left the stand.

"The defense calls Dr. Melinda Ivanov to the stand."

Melinda took her place. Bob was always impressed by her solemn expression when she took the oath. He wondered if having grown up in Russia gave her a special reverence for American justice, warts and all.

"Dr. Ivanov, you are chief medical examiner for the city of San Diego, are you not?"

"Yes."

"How long have you been in that position?"

"Twenty-four years."

"And you were out of the country at the time of Catherine Yaeger's autopsy, were you not?"

"Yes. I was in Russia. My father was terminally ill."

"When you returned, did you review Dr. Goldstein's work?"

"Yes."

"And what did you conclude?"

"That Dr. Goldstein was correct, that Catherine Yaeger's heart stopped as a result of a lethal combination of alcohol and the drug Demerol. Very few individuals could have survived that combination, in those quantities, and certainly not a young woman of Ms. Yaeger's size."

"Based on your many years of medical experience, do you believe it possible that choking during intercourse contributed to Ms. Yaeger's death?"

"I do not."

"Why not?"

"As Dr. Goldstein said, the bruises discovered in the second autopsy were minor."

"Have you ever seen death by strangulation?"

"Yes, many times."

"How many, would you say?"

"Roughly a dozen."

"In those cases, were the physical traces of strangulation different than the findings here?"

"Yes, very different."

"Thank you. Nothing further."

Bob sat.

Billy half rose out of his seat. "No questions."

The judge announced an hour recess for lunch.

79

Bob, Anna, Kenny, and his parents went to the small conference room that had been set aside for the defense. Sarah, as usual, had dropped off sandwiches and sodas.

No one spoke. Bob ate very little of his sandwich. The room was filled with tension.

Kenny's mother and Bob both left the room. Bob went to the men's bathroom and watched Mrs. Glick go into the ladies'. She looked like she was about to cry.

When the court reconvened, Bob called Robert Yaeger

to the stand.

"Mr. Yaeger, you were the father of Catherine Yaeger, is that correct?"

"Yes."

"Why did you ask for a second pathology report on her body?"

"Well, we were told the initial autopsy found accidental death. But we weren't told more than that. We wanted to know more. We wanted specifics."

"Did you subsequently learn why you had been given so little information?"

"Yes. The Chief Medical Examiner was away, and she had to review the report. Sign off on it. That hadn't happened yet."

"That would be Melinda Ivanov, who was in Russia with her dying father?"

"Yes."

"If you had been told more, that Catherine died due to a mixture of alcohol and Demerol, would you have asked for another autopsy?"

"Objection. Calls for speculation."

"Overruled. The witness will answer."

Yaeger bit his lip. "No."

"Thank you, sir."

Billy Lewis had no questions.

Bob knew that Billy's failure to ask questions of various witnesses was a bad sign for the prosecution and a good one for the defense.

Bob called Andrew Rich to the stand.

"Mr. Rich, you knew Catherine Yaeger as an actor, correct?"

"Yes. She appeared in several productions at Diversionary Theater, where I often direct."

"So would you say you knew her well?"

"Yes."

"Did you also know Kenneth Glick?"

"Yes."

"How well?"

"Not as well as I knew Cathy, but I saw them together on various occasions, at parties, that sort of thing."

"How would you describe their relationship?"

"Close, but tempestuous."

"How do you mean that?"

"I think they both had tempers. They argued a good bit, sometimes shouted at each other."

"Did both of them do the arguing, the shouting?"

"Yes."

"Did you ever see any physical violence between them?"

Rich then repeated what he had told Bob.

"I saw Cathy slap Ken hard, once, at a party. Then Ken grabbed her by the shoulders and said something to her, and she smiled. They both did. I got the sense they were like that when they were together."

"So just to be clear, Ms. Yaeger slapped Mr. Glick?"

"Yes."

"When Mr. Glick grabbed her by the shoulders, did that seem like a violent gesture?"

Billy objected. "Calls for speculation."

"Overruled."

"No, it did not."

"Were you aware of Ms. Yaeger's substance abuse problems?"

"I was aware that she sometimes drank, yes."

"Did it appear to you that she drank to excess?"

"Objection. The witness is not medically qualified to answer."

"I'll allow it."

"Yes, it did. It worried me."

"Thank you." Bob looked at the judge. "Nothing further."

Billy had no questions.

"The defense calls Peter Arnold."

He took the stand.

"Mr. Arnold, did you know Catherine Yaeger?"

"Yes."

"How did you meet?"

"We met at a party at her parent's beach house in Laguna. Mr. Yaeger is a business associate of mine."

"And did you eventually develop a sexual relationship with Catherine?"

"Yes."

"Where did these encounters take place?"

"At my house in Palm Springs, and a few times in her apartment here in town."

Bob could hear whispered remarks and a few gasps. Judge Murphy did not bang her gavel, but she looked sternly around the courtroom

"Mr. Arnold, have you ever been arrested?"

He looked away, toward the windows.

"Yes."

"On what charge?"

"Domestic battery."

There were loud murmurs this time, and twice the judge banged her gavel loudly. The courtroom grew silent.

"Who was the alleged victim?"

"My ex-wife."

"In fact the police were called to your home in Los Angeles several times due to a domestic disturbance, were they not?"

"Yes."

"How many times."

"Three."

More murmuring.

"Did you ever plead guilty to a formal charge of battery?"

"Yes."

"And what was the sentence?"

"A fine, community service, and a commitment to therapy, which I took seriously."

"Was your relationship—your sexual relationship—with Catherine Yaeger violent?"

"Not violent, no, but intense."

"How do you mean that?"

"Well, Cathy liked to be in charge. She would call me her sex slave. It was a performance. A good one. She was convincing. I think she was trying to show me she could act. I'm an executive at MGM and she wanted a career as an actor."

Then Bob thought of a question he had not asked Peters when they first met. It was always risky to ask a question of a witness out of the blue, but Bob made a split-second decision to go ahead.

"Did you ever strangle Catherine?"

"She asked me to. In a gentle way."

The judge banged her gavel again.

"How did she ask?"

"She'd say something like, 'Put your hands around my neck, slave, and press, gently.'"

"Thank you. No further questions."

Billy stood. "Mr. Arnold, did you ever give money to Catherine Yaeger?"

"She once asked to borrow $400. I gave it to her."

"Did she pay it back?"

"I don't think she had the chance."

"Nothing further."

Peters left the stand, and there was a very long pause. Everyone looked at the judge, who seemed to be thinking. Bob was about to rest his case when the judge banged her gavel and said they were done for the day.

80

As soon as Bob got back to his office, Jason walked in, looking panicked.

"What's wrong?" Bob asked.

"Boss, I messed up."

Bob closed his eyes for a moment. He knew that something was wrong when Jason called him "boss."

"How?"

"I forgot to check Richard Cartwright's alibi."

Bob swallowed hard. "And?"

"On the morning Cathy Yaeger was murdered, he wasn't at Universal studios. He was there the day before. But not that day. They didn't need him."

"Which means . . ." Bob stood up and started to pace.

"Which means he lied to you."

"Do we know anything about how he spent that day?"

"No. But, at least based on the names he gave us, he has no alibi for that day. He could have driven down here, seen Cathy, and driven back to LA. There was plenty of time. He wasn't seen again until later that evening. As far as I can tell."

"Jesus Christ. I mean, it's suspicious, but he could have been anywhere."

"I showed his picture around Cathy's apartment building." Bob stopped pacing.

"And?"

"And one tenant thought maybe he had seen him there once or twice, but couldn't remember when. Of course . . ."

"What?"

"He's an actor. He might've just looked familiar."

"Maybe. Maybe not. This certainly makes him a suspect. But what's his motive?" Bob was pacing again. "Why would he kill her?"

"Do we care? I mean, of course we care. Maybe it was sex that got out of hand. Who knows?"

"Conjecture."

"Yes, but if we can show there's another suspect, raise doubts about the police investigation . . ."

Bob was thinking the same thing. "Right. Reasonable doubt."

"So what now?" Jason asked.

Bob sat down. "We ask for a postponement and issue a subpoena."

"I'm so sorry. I really screwed up."

Bob looked at Jason. He didn't think he had ever seen him so upset. "It was a mistake. But you found it. In time. And it will shake up the jury. Maybe it's for the best."

Jason tried to smile.

Last-minute surprises at trial always worried Bob. He could end up looking desperate, throwing a curve ball. But on his way home he decided he needed to use what Jason had uncovered, to throw doubt on the police if nothing else.

Marcus had a dinner on campus that night, so Bob ordered a pizza and drank several glasses of wine. Oscar sat by Marcus's usual chair, looking confused; it was rare for one of them to have dinner at home without the other. Bob went to bed early, before Marcus got home.

The next morning when court convened, Bob asked to approach, and, when he and Billy stood before the judge, he explained what had happened. Billy objected vigorously, but the judge ordered the trial recessed for no more than 48 hours.

Bob went back to his office, quickly drew up a summons, sent Anna to get it approved by the judge, and then sent Jason to LA to deliver it.

He spent the rest of the day resting, working in the garden, and playing with Oscar on the patio, when he had a thought.

They could expand their house out the back, there was plenty of room. They wouldn't need to move. They could add a bedroom and bath, maybe a playroom.

81

The next day as soon as court reconvened, Bob rose and called Richard Cartwright to the stand. The crowd murmured—Bob heard some gasps—and the judge banged her gavel twice. While taking the oath, Cartwright glanced around the courtroom. *Looking for a good camera angle*, Bob thought. Only there were no cameras.

"Mr. Cartwright, do you recall meeting with me at your home in Los Angeles a few months ago?"

"Yes."

"And at that time, what did you tell me about your whereabouts on March eighteenth and nineteenth of last year?"

"I said that I was filming."

"But you weren't actually filming both of those days, only the first. Isn't that correct?"

"Yes."

"Were you acquainted with the deceased, Catherine Yaeger?"

"Yes."

"In fact you had an intimate encounter with her on several occasions, isn't that right?"

"Yes." Cartwright showed no signs of distress; he was either a cool customer or good at playing one.

"Your Honor, may I approach?"

Murphy nodded, and Bob walked up to the witness box.

"If you were not at the studio, where in fact were you on March nineteenth?"

"I was alone, at home, studying my script. When you questioned me, what I remembered about those days was the film I was working on, even when I was home, just studying the script."

Much murmuring. Bob could see that the judge looked surprised. So surprised, Bob realized, that she didn't bang her gavel.

"Home alone," Bob repeated.

"Yes."

Bob walked toward the jury. "Why lie about it?" Bob emphasized the word "lie."

"Because I knew how this could look."

"You say you were home alone."

Billy stood to object—the question had been asked and answered—but Cartwright responded quickly.

"Yes, I was home alone." He sounded emphatic, even angry, as if he had rehearsed the line.

Bob turned back toward the witness stand and paused,

taking a deep breath. He spoke very slowly.

"Isn't that another lie, Mr. Cartwright? Is it not the case that you drove from Los Angeles to San Diego, visited Catherine Yaeger, and murdered her?"

Billy leapt to his feet. "Objection. This man has not been accused of anything."

"No, he hasn't been," Bob said with both anger and sarcasm in his voice, turning to look directly at Billy. "Was he even investigated?" Bob knew he was breaking the rules by speaking directly to opposing counsel. He was risking a dressing-down from the judge or even a contempt citation, but he didn't stop, didn't care.

For the first time ever, he didn't care.

Judge Murphy banged her gavel and looked angry. "I will see both counsel in chambers. The witness is excused."

82

The two lawyers followed her and stood before her in her chambers as she sat at her desk. She poured herself a glass of water and took several gulps.

"Do you remember, Mr. Abramson, my instructions? No theatrics."

"I apologize, Your Honor."

"You were showboating for the jury. You know that any remarks about opposing counsel or the investigation need to be directed at me, do you not? That's law school 101. And if memory serves, you went to Harvard Law. I would guess they teach that at Harvard."

"Yes, ma'am. Again, I apologize."

"If you ever do that again in my courtroom, there will be severe consequences."

"Yes, Your Honor." Bob tried to look contrite, but he still didn't care. In fact, he felt exhilarated by what he had done.

And that frightened him.

The judge took another gulp of water and paused. The lawyers waited. Bob shifted his weight from one foot to the other. Finally, she spoke.

"I am dismissing the jury in favor of a directed verdict of not guilty."

"Your Honor, you can't." Billy burst out. He sounded genuinely panicked.

"I can and I will. This has got to be the weakest murder case I've ever seen. Or heard of. Your witnesses have been discredited. You have no real evidence. We've heard from the deceased's mother that she had a substance abuse problem. We've heard from the Medical Examiner, who, to my knowledge, has never been wrong. The deceased clearly liked intense sex."

They both could hear distaste in Judge Murphy's voice. She went on.

"At a minimum, there's no clear evidence of foul play. The police conducted a sloppy investigation, if you can even call it an investigation. They apparently neglected at least one plausible suspect. That is on them, but it's your job to review their work, judge the strength of their case."

She looked directly at Billy with fury, Bob thought. The tone in her voice would have scared Perry Mason.

Billy said nothing.

"And tell Mr. Stevens if he ever sends a case this weak to my courtroom again, I will move to have him disbarred."

"Yes, Your Honor." Billy turned bright red.

"Now let's go back in and end this farce."

They all walked back into the courtroom. Billy and Bob took their seats.

"Bailiff," the judge said, "please escort the jury and the alternates out of the courtroom."

They filed out, some looking puzzled.

Judge Murphy then said, simply and quietly, "This case is dismissed in favor of a directed verdict of not guilty."

Pandemonium erupted as the reporters dashed out to break the story.

The judge banged her gavel three times, and when there was silence, she said, "Mr. Glick, you are free to go."

She banged her gavel yet again, this time to signal that the trial was over.

Kenny sat down looking stunned. The he stood again and hugged Bob.

The courtroom emptied. Kenny's parents came up. His mother hugged him, and he told Anna and Kenny he'd catch up to them.

83

Bob and Billy gathered their papers into briefcases and walked out together, behind everyone else.

"Billy, I—"

The ADA cut him off. "Congratulations, counselor."

"Off the record, why did Fred push this?"

"I don't know. He's been making a lot of bad decisions. You know he's going through a divorce."

"No, I didn't. No wonder. That could drive anyone crazy."

"Yeah. He's moved out of the house. It hasn't hit the press yet. Anyway. You did your job. I didn't."

And with that, Billy ducked into the men's room. He looked shrunken.

Bob joined Kenny and his parents, standing with Anna in the side corridor.

"I think we should go out the back way," he said. "The press will be out front, and I don't think any of us should say anything."

"Are you sure?" Kenny asked.

"Quite sure. It's important not to gloat."

He showed them the way out. Kenny hugged him again. Anna and Bob drove back to the office.

"Were you expecting that?" Anna asked.

"No. But the judge was right. There really was no case against Kenny. Legally."

"And morally?"

Bob thought for a moment.

"I don't know. I mean there's the law, and then . . ."

"There's real life."

Bob smiled. Anna got it.

84

Back at the office Jason congratulated him and Sarah hugged him. He thanked them, closed the door to his inner office, and stared out the window for a long time.

It was still early in the day. He drove home. Marcus was working in his study, Oscar at his feet. They both came out to greet him.

Bob told Marcus what happened.

"That's wonderful. Congratulations! We should celebrate."

"I just need to sleep."

Marcus knew that was typical for Bob; he was always exhausted when he finished a high-stakes trial.

Bob took a long nap, and then they showered and went to dinner at California Cuisine. They didn't talk much over dinner. Bob asked Marcus how his writing was going.

"Well enough. It's a slog. I'm glad I took the time off."

Bob smiled.

"I've been thinking," Marcus said as they left the restaurant, "we should go ahead. Talk to the lawyer about adoption. A little girl. We'll call her Ruth."

Bob stopped walking and hugged Marcus tight. His eyes were moist.

A message was on the answering machine when they got home. It was from Kenny.

"Hey. I'm having a party tomorrow night to celebrate. At my place. I hope both of you can make it."

"Should we go?" Marcus asked.

"You can. I'll stay home."

85

The party was jammed with young people, some of whom he recognized, including a few graduate students. Rock music was blaring from the stereo, from a band Marcus didn't know, the more it played, the less he liked it. The apartment was sparsely furnished in a style Marcus thought of as early graduate student.

He felt completely out of place, but he congratulated Kenny and did his best to make small talk with some of the students. He drank cheap white wine from a box sitting on the kitchen counter. The sweetish smell of marijuana wafted through the rooms, making him feel light-headed.

Marcus could tell Kenny had had too much to drink. Unlike the sober graduate student Marcus was used to seeing, the boy was talking loudly and groping some of the women, who did their best to push him away.

After half an hour or so Marcus was ready to leave; the music and the bad wine were giving him a headache. First, though, he needed the bathroom, which was off one of the dimly lit bedrooms, through a dark, narrow alcove that had been fitted out as a makeshift closet. The alcove connected the two bedrooms, and Marcus realized he had no idea who Kenny's roommate was.

Strange floor plan, he thought.

He used the toilet and then lowered the top and sat on it for several minutes, massaging his temples, trying to get his head to stop pounding. He didn't want to go back into the living room with its blaring music.

When he finally came out of the bathroom into the dark of the alcove, Marcus could see that Kenny was in the bedroom and had a young woman in his arms. She was slender and blond and wearing a yellow halter top. They were just finishing what looked like a passionate kiss. Kenny had his hands on her rear.

And then Marcus heard the young woman say words he remembered for a long time.

"It's a good thing the Demerol worked."

86

Marcus willed himself to be calm. He walked into the bedroom, pretending to ignore Kenny and the young woman, and went quickly through to the living room and out the front door.

He was halfway down the outside stairs when he heard Kenny behind him, three steps away.

"Gee, Marky, I guess you caught me. And you can't do a thing about it."

Double jeopardy. He had been found not guilty. He couldn't be charged with the same crime.

Marcus turned around. Kenny was smirking. There was a residue of bright red lipstick on his neck.

"Why, Kenny?"

"Why? Shit. You guys, you baby boomers, you gobble up all the jobs and all the real estate and leave the rest of us with crumbs."

"Money?"

"Duh, money. You know, the stuff you need to buy food and clothes and a car and a place to live. Not a shithole like this apartment. You know how expensive it is to live here, or in LA? Work hard and play by the rules, Clinton's bullshit. Total crap. The Clintons cashed in. Like everybody else."

"Kenny, you were on your way to a PhD."

"Yeah, and what would that get me? Year after year as a temporary adjunct making peanuts, and then maybe a job in Nebraska or at a junior college in Fresno? No thank you."

For a fraction of a second, Marcus felt a pang of guilt; Kenny could have been right about his academic future. But he quickly snapped out of it.

"Your family. Her family. Both of you came from money."

"Our parents weren't going to support us forever. They made that clear. What were we supposed to do? Wait for them to die?"

"So you turned into an escort."

"We provided a service. A lot of money for not a lot of time, and hey, sometimes it was actually hot. We gave people what they wanted."

"And Cathy . . ."

"At first she was really into it. But then . . ."

"Then?"

He shrugged. "She wanted out."

"And you wouldn't let her go." Marcus felt a kind of nausea, tinged with both grief and anger.

"I trained her. She knew what to do. And hey, she was a babe. And a good actress. She attracted a lot of rich clients. And . . ."

"And?" The anger was taking over.

Kenny looked away. "She threatened to tell the police I forced her. Which is bullshit."

"She wanted out," Marcus repeated, mostly to himself.

Kenny started walking down the stairs to where Marcus had stopped. His face was contorted.

Again, Marcus forced himself to stay calm. He quickly looked up and saw two graduate students at the other end of the long landing, kissing. The boy had a cigarette in his hand.

"Jeannie, Gary, we need you over here."

Gary put out his cigarette and they both came over.

"Take Kenny back inside. He's had too much to drink. We don't want him to fall off the stairs."

They nodded, then took Kenny by both arms and moved him back up toward the open apartment door. At first he struggled against their hold but soon relented.

87

Marcus turned around and very slowly walked down the rest of the stairs, gripping the banister.

The air felt heavy. His legs felt heavy.

He walked to his car, got in, and locked the door. When he put the key in the ignition, he realized his hands were shaking slightly. He held them together until the shaking stopped.

They could charge Kenny with other crimes; Marcus knew enough law to know that. Solicitation. Pandering. Perhaps a civil suit from her parents for wrongful death.

Something. Bob can go to the DA. He'll hate it, but he'll do it.

Marcus realized a new trial of any kind would mean he'd have to testify about what he had just seen and heard.

And that meant Bob couldn't continue as Kenny's lawyer.

He drove home and parked in front of their house, closed the car windows, and rested his head on the steering wheel. Then he got out and sat down on the front stoop. He stayed there a while, smelling the night-blooming jasmine they had planted around the front of the house.

Finally he got up and went in.

He felt exhausted. He had never been afraid to tell Bob anything, but he was afraid to tell him this.

Bob was half-asleep on the couch, Oscar sprawled on the floor in front of him. They both stirred when Marcus walked in, Oscar thumping his tail on the floor. A jazz record was playing at low volume. Coltrane.

"Hey. How was the party?"

Marcus sat down, patted Oscar's head. "I have something to tell you. But first, call Jason, tell him to come over and sleep on the couch. And tell him to bring his gun."

"What?" Bob was rubbing his eyes.

"It's important. I'll explain."

"Pinky . . ."

"Call Jason." Marcus stood and pulled Bob to his feet.

Bob was bleary-eyed, but something in Marcus's tone made him do what he said. He went into the kitchen and dialed Jason and gave him Marcus's instructions.

"I can explain when you get here," Bob said into the phone. "I hope." He hung up.

Bob walked back into the living room and sat next to Marcus on the couch, who took his hand.

"So, what's this about?"

Marcus looked up and out the window. It had started to rain.

Rain

Acknowledgments

Heartfelt thanks to the indispensable editor Priscilla Long, to Ana Cara, Sandra Zagarell, and Carter McAdams, for reading drafts, and once again to A.D. Reed of Pisgah Press.

This is a work of fiction. Aside from any brief mentions of public figures, no true events or real individuals are depicted.

About the Author

H. N. Hirsch was born in Chicago and educated at the University of Michigan and at Princeton. A political scientist by training, he has been on the faculties of Harvard, the University of California-San Diego, Macalester College, and Oberlin, where he served as Dean of the Faculty and is now the Erwin N. Griswold Professor of Politics Emeritus. He is the author of *The Enigma of Felix Frankfurter* ("brilliant and sure to be controversial"—*The New York Times*), *A Theory of Liberty*, and the memoir *Office Hours* ("well crafted and wistful"—Kirkus), and numerous articles on law, politics, and constitutional questions.

About Pisgah Press

Pisgah Press was established in 2011 in Asheville, NC to publish works of quality offering original ideas and insight into the human condition and the world around us. If you support the old-fashioned tradition of publishing for the pleasure of the reader and the benefit of the author, please encourage your friends and colleagues to visit www.PisgahPress.com. For more information about *Shade* and other Pisgah Press books, contact us at pisgahpress@gmail.com.

Also available from Pisgah Press

Gabriel's Songbook — Michael Amos Cody
$17.95 FINALIST, FEATHERED QUILL BOOK AWARD, FICTION, 2021

A Twilight Reel
$17.95 GOLD MEDALIST, FEATHERED QUILL BOOK AWARD, SHORT STORIES, 2021

Letters of the Lost Children: Japan—WWII — Reinhold C. Ferster
$37.95 & Jan Atchley Bevan

Musical Morphine: Transforming Pain One Note at a Time — Robin Russell Gaiser
$17.95 FINALIST, USA BOOK AWARDS, 2017

Open for Lunch
$17.95

Fault Line   THE BOB & MARCUS MYSTERY SERIES   H.N. Hirsch
22.95
Shade
22.95
Rain
22.95

The Last of the Swindlers — Peter Loewer
$17.95

Homo Sapiens: A Violent Gene? — Mort Malkin
$22.95

Reed's Homophones: A Comprehensive Book of Sound-alike Words — A.D. Reed
$17.95

Swords in their Hands: George Washington and the Newburgh Conspiracy — Dave Richards
$24.95 FINALIST, USA BOOK AWARDS, HISTORY, 2014

Trang Sen: A Novel of Vietnam — Sarah-Ann Smith
$19.50

Deadly Dancing   THE RICK RYDER MYSTERY SERIES   RF Wilson
$15.95
Killer Weed
$14.95
The Pot Professor
$17.95
Murder on the Rocks
$22.95

To order:

Pisgah Press, LLC
PO Box 9663, Asheville, NC 28815
www.pisgahpress.com

Printed in the USA
CPSIA information can be obtained
at www.ICGtesting.com
CBHW070838120524
8286CB00009B/138